I0675160

I AM MATTHEW, THE COOPER'S SON.

(CLOSING THE (RING)

Charlotte A. Hutt

 New Generation Publishing

FOR NOAH BEAR

Notes

In 1997, while extending accommodation on the American Airbase of Lakenheath, Suffolk, the baseball pitch was dug up and the grave of an Anglo-Saxon warrior was discovered.

The warrior (on his horse) was ringed by the graves of small children. This arrangement, archaeologists decided, was unusual and without explanation. Archaeologists are still examining the bones.

Medieval Horringer was sheep country.

The Black Death of 1348 hit Suffolk, its towns and villages, very hard due to their close proximity to ports.

On the road from Bury St. Edmunds to Newmarket is Risby. Eight miles further on the right on the crossroads is an unprotected but always bedecked grave, it can be seen to this day. Here was buried a shepherd lad who, accused of stealing a sheep when such a crime carried the death penalty, hanged himself.

PROLOGUE

600 A.D.

When the Anglo-Saxon Eurith The Strong, he who was wrongly called *The First Knight*, knew his time had come, he bid the village elders to see to his burial and honour his grave. His own son had displeased him. He had not followed his father's code of honour:

HONOUR YOUR BETTERS
RESPECT YOUR PEERS
LOOK AFTER THE POOR AND DESTITUTE

His son thought no-one was better than he was, and he despised those in ill health. Therefore his father had forbidden him the village and the flatlands they inhabited and cast him out into the wilderness to perish.

The elders gave their pledge before death descended onto the knight and clouded his eyes. He would be buried according to his wishes for he was a brave knight, a protector of the children, who lived up to his motto:

THE BROTHERHOOD
IN LIFE
IN DEATH

Eurith The Strong had been baptised, but he reverted to his Pagan background.

The dead knight's wooden shield and his marvellously forged, strong sword were put into his hands after he was placed on his horse which would be buried with him in the grave. It wore the bronze and silver decorated bridle and the slim, elongated shield dangling from its neck. His band of men and the villagers gathered silently around the open grave as the sun rose over the horizon.

When it reached its highest point and the light on the decorations leapt into their eyes, they threw earth over the knight and his horse. When it was done, they dug a trench all around the grave with the knight at its centre; the knight was the sun and the children its rays.

It was the ritual as laid down by the warrior himself. In life he had been proud and wanted to be addressed as *The First Knight* even if he was a descendant of Sir Lancelot, one of the Knight Errant of the Round Table, who had roamed the world for adventure.

Lancelot's descendant had not passed on his heritage to his son. His son, cast out by him, was alive, and a curse was laid on the knight to reside in *Neitherland* forever, but he was buried in the manner of the Round Table, the eternal flame of brotherhood burning at its centre in memory of his heritage.

His daughters stood weeping amongst the other village children standing around the grave. Carrying sheaves of corn and with cornflowers woven into their long flaxen hair, some of these children would be buried around the man who was wrongly called *The First Knight*, for life was not only uncertain but also short.

I, Morgan le Fey of Avalon, half-sister of King Arthur of all the Britons, have witnessed the burial of Eurith The Strong; I was at the blue heart of the flame of eternal brotherhood.

I had abused the gift of healing bestowed upon

6

me by choosing to exercise it for those who pleased me. Or worse, I reversed the gift and stole the health of people, for I was King Arthur's dark side that came from our father, Uther Pendragon.

I, Morgan le Fey, want to make amends for my past wickedness. I will lift the curse laid on him for betraying his heritage. He will not reside in *Neitherland* for all time. He will be able to lead the children out of *Neitherland* when he is found by the one I will call *The Seeker*. This time will be when a new legend is born, one who will make the land bloom. *It has to be done before the knight's bones are taken away for all the world to see.*

The ring of history is closed when one legend dies and another one is born, for there can be no beginnings without endings.

I shall appoint the boy who will be the Seeker. It will be a hard task, for the boy will have free will and yet he will have to fulfil his destiny, but I have the help of Merlin, the last of the magicians. He will not refuse me aid, for I am Morgan le Fey, half-sister of Arthur, King of all the Britons.

BOOK I:

THE SEEKER

Chapter 1

The hour had arrived. I was called forth from *Neitherland* as it had been foretold.

I was about to finish my set task when I heard a boy who was crying.

Jacob!

Jacob had been my friend, and the crying came from above. I threw myself headlong into the dark place above me.

When I emerged from the yew tree, I blinked; I had been ejected from *Neitherland's* darkness into daylight. I could not adjust to my new surroundings. My vision distorted everything into many shapes, one of which wailed like an old dog in a ditch.

When I had crossed over into Camelot, the obscure world had not revealed itself until I had washed myself in the river of time.

I now touched the magic blue ribbon, the ribbon of time given to me by Morgan le Fey, and the world before me sprang into sharp focus.

I walked from the old yew tree from where I had risen towards the apple tree leaning heavy with white blossom. The sky was a watery blue, so I knew it was springtime.

'I'm Edwin. Who are you?' the boy who had been crying asked.

'I am Matthew, the cooper's son. Where are we? What year is it?' I asked Edwin.

'We're in Suffolk, in England, and this is 1997,' he replied, wiping his nose.

'EEDWIIIN!'

Somebody was calling from the house.

'Just a minute,' he cried and got up.

'Are you just leaving me here?' I asked.

He looked at me with horror.

I wasn't too pleased myself; I was fading into the apple tree I had meant to lean against. It is disturbing to see the inside of a tree when you are not expecting it.

'Are you a hallucination?' Edwin asked me when I was clear of the tree. Although I understood and spoke the language of the England of Edwin's day since I had touched the blue ribbon of time, I made a note of this strange new word *hallucination*.

I always liked long words and I was often told I had a big mouth.

'Why are you talking to yourself, Edwin?' said a person coming down the garden.

'So I know what I'm talking about,' Edwin said.

The speaker addressing Edwin was a short-legged, plump man with tight, grey curly hair. He wore flowered breeches and a tunic - as bright as a butterfly - reaching his knees.

His voice was high-pitched, and he smelled like a chamber filled with flowers.

'You have to be a good boy, Edwin,' this strange person said. 'Stop hiding your mother's shoes. It won't prevent her from going away.'

'All right, grandma,' he said.

Then he turned to me.

'I'll be back,' he shouted at me, 'just like The Terminator.'

As I didn't like the sound of whoever that might be, I made no note of this strange word.

The odd person in the flowered breeches was *the boy's grandmother*, dressed like a colourful man, but why?

I have learned since that girls and women were all attired like men, or worse, some were so scantily dressed, I wanted to cover them up with a horse blanket, if they still had them.

I learned the way of Edwin's age while I waited for him to return to this place after he came back with his mother.

I learned that the sad, solitary man walking in the garden and talking to himself - very often with something he pressed against his ear - was Edwin's father.

Sometimes he tried to set fire to himself with a straight twig he set alight in his mouth, time after time. I hoped the family would unite before he burst into flames.

Maybe it was a penance, like the woolhard, the hairshirt the Blessed Abbot had worn when he had repented.

Sometimes the boy's grandmother arrived in a covered red cart that moved without the aid of a horse but with four madly spinning wheels.

Edwin's father had a large silver cart.

He spent a lot of time washing it down, drying it with a cloth and walking round it admiringly, and he stabled it nightly.

I decided the cart had taken the place of the horse when, to my joy, I heard the happ-happ-happ-happy canter of a horse from a lane beyond the hedge bordering the garden. It pleased me that horses still had four legs and not four wheels, but I stayed where I was, waiting for Edwin. I needed his help if I was to return to *Neitherland* and complete my task for I needed Edwin's help.

Chapter 2

Suddenly life returned to the house and spilled into the garden. Edwin ran outside to see if I was still there, as indeed I was. We talked together, and although I was what Edwin called *insubstantial*, the ground under my feet did not give way, I could not find my way back to my friends Mattie and Frog and the knight who were still residing in *Neitherland*.

'You're looking for a different dimension,' Edwin cried. 'Look on the world as a giant spider's web; it vibrates to the outer edges when the centre is disturbed.'

'So?'

'So we have to find the centre of the disturbance and fling you back where you came from.'

Merlin himself had reached that conclusion. But more to the point, what did Edwin's parents think when he was talking to himself, or worse-laughing? After all, they could not see me.

'They're talking about sending me to a child psychologist,' he said glumly. We were talking in his bed chamber. 'Getting my head examined.'

It was a good head. He had a fine-featured face with a high forehead hidden under floppy blonde hair.

'But I shan't go,' he added.

'You will have to do as your parents wish. You have to honour your father and your mother. It's one of the Ten Commandments.'

Edwin scratched his head.

'The Ten Commandments are not the Ten Suggestions.' I added. I had been told that myself.

'Right, it's from the Bible. My father doesn't believe in God,' said Edwin.

'Every Catholic believes in God.'

'My father isn't Catholic, he is American and

14

he is a Baptist. My mother is Church of England.'

'How about the Pope?'

'Oh, he is Catholic all right.'

I was pleased to hear it.

'I expect everybody had to believe in God in whatever century you come from. What century was it?'

When I told him I wasn't sure, he asked me when my birthday was.

'My birthday was on All Souls Day,' I said.

'What year?'

'Every year.'

He laughed.

'And my Saint's day, St Matthew, was on the twenty-first day of September in the sixth month of the year.'

'Ninth month,' he said.

'Doesn't the new year start on the first of April when the earth wakes up?'

'Not now it doesn't. It starts on the first of January, but never mind. Who was on the throne in your time?'

'He was an Edward; the third Edward was King in 1330, when my mother was in Clare. She told me.'

'So it was the fourteenth century,' said Edwin.

'Thirteenth.'

'Fourteenth. You see, the first hundred years, from nought to a hundred, is the first century.'

He certainly had some weird ideas, especially about the age I came from.

'The fourteenth century? Wasn't that medieval?' he asked.

'I hope I do not espy an 'evil' in that name. It was a good age to live in, apart from the dreadful disease, but I can't put a name to it yet it was so dreadful. I thought the world was coming to an end, but it can't have done.'

'Why not?'

I looked at him.

'BECAUSE YOU'RE STILL HERE!'

He laughed.

'Never thought of it.'

I asked him what they worried about in his age.

Edwin thought for a minute.

'Passive smoking, I suppose, and the icecaps. They're melting.'

I didn't understand that but it sounded dangerous. My Aunt Biddy would have burned some herb or other for the purification.

'I always thought people in medieval times cowered in mud huts and lived on gruel, whatever that is,' he said. 'They were filthy dirty and had lots and lots of children they couldn't remember the names of and who died just as soon as they were born. And they were absolutely miserable, no laughing or anything.'

If Edwin was to be of help to me, the errors of his ways would have to be pointed out to him.

He was eleven years old and he was still at school.

It was getting stranger; everybody lived in a house with many rooms, all of them labelled.

One room was used for living, one room for sitting, one room for dining, one room for washing yourself, one room for studying, and rooms were for sleeping in.

But the light they had!

They could conjure up light by touching the wall or switch, as Edwin called it.

I amused myself by turning the light on and off several times without touching the switch.

'Some sort of different energy, I suppose,'

Edwin said. 'Just a minute.'

He ran out of the room.

'Da-aa-aa-d!' he shouted down the stairs. 'What's the name of the energy that moves things without touching them?'

'Psycho-kinetic, Edwin,' his father replied almost without pausing.

'Maybe it's because you are...' Edwin struggled for words when he returned. 'Maybe it's because you are an imprint of your personality.'

I made note of that word.

'Why aren't you asking *me* any questions?' he wanted to know.

'I used to ask so many questions, Brother Aloysius used to say he would make a philosopher out of me.'

'I'll come to philosopher in a minute,' Edwin said. 'It is relevant. We used to live on the American base in Lakenheath. It's in England but we used dollars in the shops and played baseball, not cricket, that'll tell you.'

Or not, I thought.

'But they won't for much longer, they want to build some new houses on the pitch,' Edwin continued.

Edwin's father had apparently been a fighter pilot - a flyer of these monsters in the sky - and then he had monitored the airspace, whatever that was, after the Gulf war.

'He flew strategic missions', Edwin continued. 'The war was in the Middle East.'

'In the East?' I was surprised to hear it was still going on.

'Anyway,' Edwin said, 'my father says he might find some answers about peace in philosophy.'

'Excalibur is the sword of peace but it was lost when it was handed back to the lady in the lake, that's all I know about peace.'

'But now to matters in hand,' said Edwin.

I told him I had to get back to *Neitherland* before the warrior's bones were taken away for the all the world to see.

'I'll help you get back,' Edwin cried. 'But first you must tell me how you got here. And start at the very beginning.'

Where was the beginning? And did he know anything about Camelot? I asked him.

He had heard of Camelot, of the Knights of the Round Table and of King Arthur and Queen Guinevere. And he had heard of Merlin.

'I believe Merlin was a legendary wizard,' he said.

'Merlin was the last of the Druid Magicians,' I said, 'he told me so himself.'

'He can't have done, Merlin was much earlier than medieval, but in any case, it's nothing but a myth,' he said.

'It's a legend,' I told him. 'A myth is invented, but a legend is based on the truth, but I can't tell you *everything* about Camelot.'

'Why not?'

'*Because I don't know everything*,' I said.

'That's reasonable, but I'll help you get back, never fear,' cried Edwin.

'You have to be patient and let me think back to where it all started, for nothing can come of nothing.'

'Right, you have the starting point,' he cried.

**

I am Matthew, the cooper's son. The following is the story of my life as I told it to the boy Edwin. I needed his help, or I could be lost forever. *It was he* who made me come to his age with his pitiful wailing. And yet I was grateful; I had found a friend to help me in this strange, new, England where the skies had been conquered and day-light was conjured in the night.

I have learned there are only two important questions to ask in life if you are puzzled or unsure. *What is it? What does it mean?* But you have to be brave, for the answers can be hard to take. The answers also have to come from the heart.

Chapter 3

I am Matthew the cooper's son and I am nearly twelve years old.

I should be grown up and out and about in the world, but I have had many illnesses which held me back. Once I was so ill I could not move my body, apart from blinking my eyes.

But now I had recovered my health and the use of my body, I would have to go to the blacksmith and learn his trade. I didn't want to become his boy; there was bad blood between our families.

My father was no longer a cooper.

Some time ago and in the depths of winter, he had found the Lord of the Manor of Horringer who had been thrown from his horse. He had carried him for a whole day, for the Lord was a heavy man, and he had saved his life.

He was not beholden to the Manor and could come and go as he pleased.

He might have been a cooper once, long ago, but now he was an occasional shepherd, sometimes a trader, and sometimes he just disappeared. He was looking for his lost boy. How can you lose a boy? That is a mystery.

Brother Aloysius, an Austin Friar from Clare, had visited strange lands. I asked him if he had seen the Dog-people who had human bodies but heads like dogs, or the headless people whose faces were on their chests, but he hadn't.

'Would you have killed them when you saw them?' I asked him, but he said no, 'Just because people are different doesn't mean we have to kill them.'

'These are but rumours from your father, I expect,' he said. If he had met any, he would have shown them how to walk in God's grace.

He told me of strange floor coverings called carpets brought by Eleanor of Castille from a land called Spain when she married King Stephen in Anno Domini 1254, not yet one hundred years ago. Carpets were rich in colour and soft as a newly mown meadow to walk on. Maybe they had them at King Arthur's court, I thought in the evening when my mother told me the tales of King Arthur by the light of a fire.

I liked the story of the Wasteland the best.

'When King Arthur ruled the land it was a time of peace and plenty,' my mother said. 'Britain was flourishing everywhere under his rule, except in one part. King Pelham, he who ruled the land, was wounded. It was said Morgan le Fey had wrought an evil charm on him which left his wound festering. She was a great healer but she was estranged from her half-brother Arthur and she did not wish him well.'

At this point my father - if he was there - would ask my mother not to fill my head with nonsense.

'Tisn't nonsense like your dog-people,' she usually said. 'It's a legend, not a myth.'

'What is the difference?' I asked my mother once.

'A legend is based on the truth, but a myth is a made-up story,' she said.

Nobody could make up a tale like she told me of the Holy Grail kept in King Pelham's castle.

The Holy Grail had been desecrated, it was the reason for the king's ill health, and why the sun no longer rose in the morning nor the moon at night.

The fire's flames fanned out its red and yellow tongues, painting pictures of a castle with turrets and beautiful ladies wearing robes in all manner of colours, and pictures of King Arthur's knights riding out in search of the wounded King Pelham and the Holy Grail.

Lancelot, his armour shining silver like early morning light, first entered the castle. But he was not pure for one of the serving maids was made to look like King Arthur's Queen, Guinevere, who the knight had taken a liking to. He was never shown the Holy Grail. He rode away the next day over barren land and he was cursed by the starving people.

Percival found the castle next. He had been working in the castle's kitchen. He was good and obedient, but he was always asking interminable questions.

When he became a squire at the King's Court he learned their code of honour:

HONOUR YOUR BETTERS
RESPECT YOUR PEERS
LOOK AFTER THE POOR AND DESTITUTE

He was also taught to keep his own council, so when he saw the Holy Grail he never asked any questions and he failed to make the land bloom.

It was Sir Galahad, the third knight, he who was Lancelot's son, who entered the magic castle and tried to solve the riddle.

'What is the Grail? What is it for?' asked Sir Galahad when it was shown to him.

'It is the cup that caught Christ's blood after his side was pierced by a lance. The Grail will heal the king and make the land bloom,' a far-off voice said.

When King Pelham let the knight see the Grail's power, its shining grace was too much for Sir Galahad. He dropped dead on the spot, and Percival became the Keeper of the Holy Grail.

King Pelham recovered his health and the Wasteland bloomed.

Sir Galahad was a sacrifice, I realised that much.

'I will never go on a quest if it's that difficult,' I cried.

'A quest has to be difficult,' my mother said, and my aunt Biddy told me it was hardly likely I would have to go on a quest in Horringer.

Horringer was a large, spread-out village. Sheep dotted the green meadows right up to the forest. When my father was on his travels I helped Thomas, the shepherd minding the sheep.

Sheep - awkward, strong, with a temper as black as their faces and a mind as devious as their curly horns - liked nothing better than to run into the thorns of the ancient blackthorn hedge and make our lives a misery.

I wasn't strong enough to hold them with my crook but my piercing whistling served as an alarm to summon Thomas.

Today - *this is when I start my story properly so you had better pay heed-* my whistling fetched Matilda, the blacksmith's eldest daughter. She ran down from the knell where she had tethered her goats.

'I'm not whistling for you,' I said. 'So you can just go back and sit on your milking stool and look out for flying pigs.'

She always made me feel that way.

'Not Matilda again,' my mother said when I got home as night fell, feeling cross.

My mother was a spinner. We washed the wool in the stream in the summer. In the winter it froze stiffer than boards. There was fat left in it to keep the rain off when knitted into shawls and blankets by the village women

'Your hands will be as soft a girl's,' my father said when he returned in the evening with a sack of barley and found me winding the spun wool into hanks. My father was limping. He had been bitten by a fox and his right leg had gone dead on him.

I ran for some fresh nettles. They are easily found in the dark. They aren't supposed to sting if you grasp them firmly but nobody had told them that yet.

My aunt Biddy, my mother's sister, pounded them with her pestle and mortar until the juices ran green. Then she mixed it with hot pig's fat. My father winced when Biddy slammed the hot poultice on his leg. His blue eyes looked around to take his mind off the pain, scratching his head until his dark hair stood up like a halo around his square face.

'I heard a tale there'll be taxes to pay soon to fund King Edward's war. The sheriffs will take a poll, and every peasant has to pay a tax for the pleasure of breathing in,' he said.

'He'll not get it without a struggle, for folks aim to breath out as well,' Biddy said.

'What war?' I asked. King Edward must have liked fighting, there was always a war going on somewhere.

'Fighting in Europe is the best place for him. He'll take my spindle next,' my mother said.

When I asked her what the king wanted with her spindle she gave me a sharp look.

'We are talking about taxes. Honestly Matthew, sometimes I think a sheep can follow a conversation better than you do,' said Biddy.

They understand my whistling, I thought, but it wasn't wise to argue when my father was in a mood.

It looked like the sheep would have to hear it again the next day. When I woke up my father was gone, the feeling must have returned to his leg. When I realised my father had left his coat behind I ran after him, past the cottages and the village green

'He's gone to run a few errands for me. Might as well be him,' said Thomas when I ran up the hill. 'He's harder to hold than a handful of bumblebees.' He looked at me hopefully but I didn't laugh, he always said that.

'My father is just like the dog,' I said when I got home. 'He likes to roam.'

Boy is what I called the dog I had found in the woods. He was black and brown, came up to my knees, had a pointed face nothing like a hound whatsoever, and green eyes, but villagers didn't keep dogs, Biddy had said.

'Our masters keep hounds for hunting, I've heard ladies keep lapdogs, and you look neither a master nor a lady.'

Biddy ruled the roost. Her hair used to be black, she told me once, but it turned white after the ague that took her father and two of her brothers in the space of a week.

That was in the time of the great flood when food was scarce. My mother was known as the fair Elena and was in service to a wool merchant in Clare where she learned the letters and the tales of Camelot. She returned afterwards to be with her sister and mother who was never the same again

Whatever that was, I thought.

For as long as I had known her, my grandmother was looked after and fed and moved into the sun on the doorstep on a nice day and away from the fire when it got too hot.

Biddy never married on account of the tragedy, which turned her mind towards healing. She dried herbs which were hanging in great aromatic bunches from the rafters.

I found out many things my family didn't want me to know by pretending to be asleep at night, but this was the first time I asked outright what had caused the bad blood between us and the blacksmith.

Apparently my mother had been betrothed to him when my father came to the village. He was a cooper and worked at the smithy. When my mother broke with the smith and married the cooper instead, the blacksmith didn't like it much.

He was a giant of a man with a rare temper.

'He held your father over the fire and threatened to burn his face off, so he promised him his son as an apprentice when he was ten years old,' she said.

'I do not blame him,' I cried, feeling brave, I was already twelve years old -having been so ill- so I didn't have to go. 'I would promise anything not to get my face burned off.'

'No use thinking you can alter the past,' Biddy said.

How about the future? I thought, for today is yesterday's tomorrow. Or was it the other way round? I gave up thinking about it and directed my thoughts towards the blacksmith before I finally fell asleep.

Chapter 4

Our hut was made of logs, the walls filled in with mud; it was high and large but cosy. The hearth was in the middle with a smoke hole in the roof, cooking pots were suspended from chains with hooks from the ceiling onto the fire.

Wood and kindling, and a chest with our clothes were stored on the long side facing the door. At one end of the room were the table, a bench and a chair for my grandmother, and the shelves for our plates and mugs. On the other side were our sleeping places, sacks filled with straw and covered by blankets and furs, under a platform reached by a short ladder.

Biddy slept up there and sorted out her herbs.

She grumbled about pains in her legs when she climbed up and I wished she gave up climbing the ladder on account of her pains getting worse so I could sleep up there.

I have confessed this sin but I hadn't really ever repented because I wanted her space but now I was truly sorry; I dreaded living at the blacksmith's.

The blacksmith's house was made from blue-grey flint hewn out of a place called Grimes Graves. It was in the middle of the great forest stretching from the right of our village into all eternity, it seemed to me.

I intended to ask Brother Aloysius how big the forest was when he rode into our village on his old, grey horse.

He always stopped for the night and compared herbs and their growing seasons and places with Biddy. I would have liked it if Brother Aloysius had been my father, but he was not of this world. After he was crossed in love, he had taken an oath of chastity, poverty and obedience and lived in the Priory in Clare.

Last time he visited he said he did not know what he would do when his old horse died on him.

'We have got comfortable with each other,' he said, but as he had not been for some time, maybe he no longer had a horse, or maybe it was too cold.

My mother fretted in the winter that was the wasteland, but it would soon be spring.

'We will have to go and see Brother Aloysius and ask him if the good Brothers will take you at their school, Matthew,' she said.

It was a long way to Clare and my mother was not in good health, but her resolve was unshaken; she wanted to get me into the school.

I had to wash myself thoroughly, even those places the sun never shines on.

The next day I woke early. After I had thrown some wood onto the embers, red sparks bloomed in the darkness like flowers. It pleased my vanity, for I had never lost a fire. After we had breakfasted on Biddy's porridge, we all knelt and prayed that we would be met with love and understanding in Clare.

Or not, I added silently. I had no wish to live among strangers who would talk to me in Latin; Anno Domini, the only Latin words I knew, would not get me very far.

We dressed carefully for the excursion.

Spring was late this year and it was still cold. My mother wore two dresses and wound a big shawl twice around her. I wore breeches, jerkin, hat and the great coat his father left behind when he disappeared into the woods. It was too long for me but I shortened it by tying a rope around my middle.

Clutching stout walking-sticks, we made good time at first, but my mother's cough got worse and she was soon exhausted. It had rained a lot that winter; the whole world was made of mud. The rain fell like knives. We walked slowly, pulling up our boots with great squelching heaves.

I was cold and wet when we approached Clare.

'Look,' she cried, just as the evening sun broke through the grey, low clouds.

Clare laid about a thousand yards in front, or rather it seemed to float. Enclosed by meres on three sides since the flood, the sun's reflection on the water transformed the milky light into something magical, playing on a majestic castle twinkling with gold.

'It is Camelot,' I cried. I could almost see King Arthur and his Queen and her ladies, but the people on the street were ordinary maids carrying baskets and stable lads leading horses, and the buildings of the priory, the cloister, the school and the church were grey stone.

The brother peering at us through the peephole at the Priory's door didn't recognise my mother. Enveloped by her black shawl he could only see her nose and her mouth. Nor could he know how clean I had been because now I was covered in mud.

'I taught Matthew to read and write, Brother Anselm, and he has a great thirst for knowledge,' my mother said to him, but the door closed before I could say I also had some Latin.

'How rude,' my mother said, unwinding the shawl from her head, shaking her hair loose.

The door opened once more.

'Is it really you, Elena?'

My mother stood back on her heels, hands outstretched, a broad grin on her face.

'Indeed, and this is my son, Brother Anselm.'

'You are a sight for sore eyes,' Brother Anselm said, 'and I'm certain he is a fine lad under all those clothes.'

'Things are not going well here,' he said. 'Some

of the priests are causing us a deal of trouble, no preaching in the great church for Austin Friars, oh dear me, no. And the school is closing for a lack of a benefactor before it has even opened.'

The de Veres were in financial difficulties, he added.

To cap it all, his old bones were brittle as dead wood and the Abbot was gravely ill.

I knew about the Abbot. He had been a wealthy man, enjoying his life and squandering his wealth. Never having met any rich men, I did not know the details.

One day he entered a church.

On espying the crucifix, he felt pains in his hands and feet and he fell down in a swoon. He repented, wearing a hair shirt causing his back to bleed, and eventually he became the Blessed Abbot

Now he was swollen up something chronic with an evil ague, Brother Anselm said.

'Like a grape,' he added as he scurried painfully along to find Brother Aloysius.

'What is a grape?' I asked Brother Aloysius when we met him.

'Questions, questions, never seen a boy like you for questions. We'll make a philosopher out of you yet,' he cried, leading us to the Priory's guest house.

'Sit by the fire and warm yourself. I have worried about you, Elena,' he said to my mother, 'but I'm still making friends with my new horse. The poor beast has been very badly treated.'

He lifted his white habit and showed us his bruised legs.

'At least you know what will ease them, you being a healer,' I said.

Brother Aloysius thanked me for my concern and showed me his workshop.

Herbs were powdered and contained in glass phials and earthenware pots which lined one wall.

And leeches.

'They will soon be busy with the Blessed Abbot,' he said.

Before he went to tend to him, catching the leeches falling like ripe plums onto a plate, he brought us a meal from the refectory. Bacon, eggs, a meat pie and some grapes, the sweetest tasting fruit in the world.

I wouldn't mind taking a vow of poverty myself, I thought later, sitting in front of the fire listening to the soft murmuring of voices.

Brother Aloysius had heard of my father last when he had been in a fight in Bury St. Edmunds and had been shut out of the city gates.

'He's a good man who repents the past. He wants to make amends towards his lost son,' he said. 'I will pray for him.'

My father was a mystery.

He was a good man obsessed by the past who got into a fight and had lost a son, I thought, before I drifted off to sleep.

Brother Aloysius took my mother and me to the church the next day for Holy Communion.

'Matthew knows the Three Marys under the cross, the twelve Apostles, and the responses,' my mother said.

Brother Aloysius said he was not turning me into an altar boy. My mother needed me.

'You are a good son to her,' he said, but he fetched a priest, a portly old man, to perform a special mass because my mother was a good woman, well-loved here. He knew my father was a wanderer.

The church was plain barring a crucifix painted in muted colours, but the priest and two blond boys performed a sacred ritual behind the altar screen, transforming the building into a place of mystery.

The priest chanted, 'Ihentribio ad alatare Dei,' and the altar boys responded with 'Ad deum qui laetificate juventum' as my mother had taught me, but now I understood that they were question and answer, as in a quest.

''I didn't go to confession,' I told the priest when we emerged, 'because you left the church.'.

The priest rocked on his heels.

'Hmm,' he said, favouring me with a wicked look. 'As long as you remember, Matthew, that the Ten Commandments are not the Ten Suggestions.'

'Didn't they know religion was serious?' I whispered to my mother.

'I think they are trying to show you that religion doesn't have to be fought over,' she whispered back.

The priest and Brother Aloysius shook their heads and smiled, it did seem they were good men and tolerant of each other, although not every Austin Friar was.

I would find that out very shortly. If he had been a kinder brother, I sometimes wonder if what happened next would ever have taken place.

**

Edwin's place

When I paused, Edwin showed me his notes. I had only learnt letters and not what he called punctuation, so I asked him to read it to me.

'It didn't only sound interesting,' I said, 'it also led me onto what came next, returning from Clare.'

'For nothing can come of nothing,' Edwin cried. He was getting the idea, I would continue the next day.

I trotted through the kitchen where Edwin's grandmother was boiling water to drink. The amount of boiling water they consumed! I was surprised their insides hadn't shrivelled up completely.

'Oh, hello. Who are you?' she asked me.

'I am Matthew, the cooper's son,' I said, 'I am Edwin's friend.'

'First I've heard of it,' she said, turning to the window.

She clapped her hands to her face and ran into the garden, where Edwin's father was doing his penance with the stick on fire.

'Oh, my God! *He had no reflection*,' she said.

'Who?'

'Edwin's friend.'

'What friend? He is alone in the house.'

'I know, and if I wasn't so sensible, I would say he is Edwin's imaginary friend,' she said to him. 'I was out of my right mind with worry, that might account for my seeing him.'

'What was he like?'

'A teenager, I suppose. Tall, good-looking. Dark hair held in a ponytail with a blue ribbon. He wore a white shirt without a collar - a smock I suppose - woollen trousers, a dark leather jerkin, black boots.'

'And no reflection. A ghost?' Edwin's father said. 'Ghosts wear white sheets over their heads and moan, Ahhhhhhhhh,Ahhhhhhhhhhhhhh, Ahhhhhhh.'

He stopped and coughed.

'In any case it's not yet Halloween, All Souls Day, as it used to be. Would the ghost boy be trick or treat?'

'Treat, definitely, if I were fourteen again,' she cried.

If I'd had any blood it would have run cold. I was not

33

only born on All Souls Day, but my most severe agues had fallen on me on that day.

I walked down the garden and sat beneath the apple tree waiting for another day. It gave me time to gather my thoughts and direct them back to Clare, where my mother and I were getting ready for the journey back to Horringer.

Chapter 5

Matthew

We left Clare at noon knowing my prayer had been answered. I could not go to the school because there wasn't one because of the de Veres, and we had been met with love and understanding.

'Who are the de Veres?' I asked my mother.

Apparently an old and rich family, they had both built and endowed the monastery.

So it belonged to them. How odd, how could you own a religious building?

Travelling back to Horringer, we sat on cushions and we were covered by blankets in a flat cart drawn by a strong horse, guided by a bad-tempered brother from the Priory.

'Put a beggar on a horse and he rides to the devil, if you ask me,' he cried after a while.

'Nobody asked him,' my mother said, 'he means riding instead of walking is above our station.'

'Out!' cried the brother. 'The two of you. I'll give you eating the Blessed Abbot's grapes.'

We jumped off, the brother turned the cart round in the mud - with some difficulty, I was pleased to note - and vanished into the distance towards Clare.

So we walked the rest of the way in the sunshine. Soon the lanes would be a white foam of cow parsley reaching my chin. Buttercups would burst out yellow as butter and poppies would zing scarlet in the gentle green meadows.

Night soon fell, but we walked on following a path the moon illuminated like a winding ribbon. We stopped when the silvery light became obscured by wispy purple clouds. We were in danger of ending up in a mere and getting covered in leeches sucking our blood, like they did the poor Blessed Abbot's.

Or even worse, the Fishman..

The Fishman, an enormous, one-eyed man covered in scales would come out of the mere and suck out our souls.

We rested behind a tree, and I sat so close to my mother that I could feel her heart beating fast in this shrouded place. She told me the rest of King Arthur's story to chase away my terrors.

'When King Arthur fell out with Lancelot, he fought him in a country called France,' my mother said softly. 'In Arthur's absence, his kingdom fell into many factions, fighting each other. When he returned to Britain, he was old and he grew weary. He rested by a lake and his sword Excalibur was returned by one of his knights to a white hand rising from the water. That was the Lady in the Lake.'

'Who was she?' I asked, but my mother did not know.

Water. I would not have liked to live in a lake like that lady or the Fishman, when -to our horror- he came towards us. He had to be tall. In the darkness, his one yellow eye flickered searchingly above us and from side to side.

My mother crossed herself and I threw myself into his path.

'Stand and fight,' I cried, 'you one-eyed devil.'

'Give over, you damn-foolish boy,' cried Biddy, brandishing a flaming torch. She had come to meet my mother. 'How dare you give me such a fright!'

Chapter 6

'Thank God they wouldn't have you at the school,' she said later, 'it's a most un-Christian night to be out alone for your mother.'

She called me a brave boy, and I couldn't stop thinking I had called her a one-eyed devil and she had praised me for it.

My grandmother woke up briefly.

'Thank you, Lord, for giving us a new day,' she said - which Biddy took for a good omen - so I didn't laugh. In any case, the old had to be respected for having lived so long.

Biddy sniffed at her herbs and decided on an inhalation, as she called it, of comfrey to comfort us after our ordeal, as like cured like.

I didn't want any; I was content to lie in front of the hearth still in my dirty clothes. I recalled walking in the night on the path unwinding before us as I watched the fire, waiting for the flames to reveal their secret blue heart.

My mother had said I had a thirst for knowledge and to be honest, that was the first I had heard of it.

What I really hungered for in the drab mud-world of winter was colour. Bright colour. Colour lifting my spirit.

**

It was odd.

I was still walking steadily on the winding path towards a light beckoning me onward. The path turned and twisted and led me out into a land; my vision distorted into many similar elongated shapes.

My eyes were clouded by sleep, I decided, so I

cleaned my face in the wide river flowing before me. Then I noticed how dirty I was, covered in mud from my journey to Clare. I threw off my shirt, jumped into the water and washed all the dirt off.

Dressed once more and sitting on my heels, I suddenly saw the countryside of gentle meadows and meandering streams clearly.

The blue river I had washed in reflected pollarded willows in its clear waters and it ran through the land like a ribbon.

Now in the day luminous with sunshine, I watched golden fish jumping with joy over bright flower heads of water buttercups.

Then I heard light, silvery voices, and I glimpsed a tantalising blue out of the corner of my eyes.

I rose and broke into a run, trying to catch the blue lady riding ahead of me, but however fast I ran I could not quite catch up with her until she slowed down.

The lady had a haughty face with a high forehead. Her golden hair was elaborately braided and wound about her head in a cone from which a soft blue veil flowed right down her back. She was dressed in a rich gown of the same blue and she dangled a blue ribbon in front of my eyes. She sat sideways on a most beautiful pale grey horse with a white mane and tail.

It shook its head and snorted.

'Steady on, Moonshine,' said the lady, and reined it in.

'There is someone I have a mind to converse with. It is this pretty boy,' she said to her companions, pointing at me.

All the lovely ladies were seated on horses, and all were dressed in richly embroidered and colourful robes of red, yellow and green, the likes of which I had never seen and which made me nearly dizzy.

'What a pretty boy. Back as straight as a sapling. Skin as fair as a lily. Hair as dark as night, and then there's his eyes.' She paused. 'Now what colour would they be called? Hazel, methinks.'

'Hazel is not a colour, it is a nut,' I said. I did not like to be talked about as if I were an object for their amusement.

'What is your name, my pretty?'

'Matthew.'

She made me feel like a girl, maybe I looked like one in my bleached linen shirt, I thought as I looked about me.

In the distance, I saw a shimmering castle with guardian towers rising from a spreading forest and green fields. It was a castle and a landscape just as my mother had described them, except for one thing; a bright banner was fluttering from the castle's main tower in the breeze, the same breeze that caressed my face and tugged at white clouds floating in the azure sky.

It had to be real, it had to be...

'Is this really Camelot?' I asked.

'Just so.'

'Are you Queen Guinevere?'

'Do I wear a crown?' she countered. 'Do I ride a white horse? Do I have a page leading it?'

It was a roundabout way of saying no, she was not, I decided.

The lady paused.

'He does not ask the right questions, my good ladies,' she said. 'That could be a worry. The last two boys were sore disappointments to me.'

'Who are you?'

'That's better,' the lady cried. 'I am Morgan le Fey, and these lovely creatures are my ladies. Do you think my ladies and I are pretty, the prettiest you have ever seen?'

'You are all very handsome, but my mother is prettier,' I said.

Not as pretty as his mother,' Morgan le Fey said to her ladies, as if I wasn't there.

'Well said, Matthew,' she added after a while, 'very well said. I like a boy who champions his mother. I think this might be the boy we have been waiting for all this time. But let us ask him the question first,' she added, turning to her ladies.

'Have you washed in the river of time?' she asked.

'Not completely. I could never put my head under the water.'

'No matter, as long as you only washed and not completely immersed yourself. I mean you do want to keep on growing, don't you?'

'Too right!'

'Now listen most carefully, Matthew. You have been chosen.'

'Chosen? Me? To do what?' I asked.

'I cannot tell all.'

'Why not?'

She sighed and shook her head at me irritably.

'I cannot tell all because I do not know all. Suffice to say that you have to perform some tasks. I have been let down by the first two boys and now the tasks are more complex.'

Her ladies drew around her in support.

'Find the Last Knight who was not the Last Knight.
Do not turn back the dragon's breath.
Find the nobleman who is not a nobleman.
Find the First Knight who was not the First

Knight.'

She repeated the task slowly and clearly.

'You will have help to tread the right path and fulfil your destiny but I cannot help it that you have a will of your own. It used to annoy me, but I realise you will need it as I do not know anything about the last task.'

'Where have the tasks come from?'

'Partly from me and partly from the master. I have had to ask for his help even though he is very weary and preserving his strength. Two tasks were added when the two boys failed. You must take great care not to forget what I said. Here, catch hold of the blue ribbon. It is the ribbon of time. Take care and never lose him.'

Even as I wondered why she addressed the ribbon as *him* it flew towards me and wound itself around my wrist.

'The ribbon of time is part of the dragon's breath. What do you think it means?'

'Absolutely nothing.'

'You will know when the time comes. Do you want to ask me anything?'

'Who is the lady in the lake? The one to who Excalibur was returned? Only my mother didn't know.'

The lady laughed, a bright, silvery laugh.

'It was the Queen of the Fairies, tell your mother. But the important thing is that Excalibur is the sword of peace. Do you wish to know more?'

'What was the Round Table made out of? I know it was round so nobody could be more important than anybody else.'

'Just so, Matthew, and it was made up of the knights' shields. But the place of the Siege Perilous was empty and so the ring was incomplete. Do you

41

know what a ring is?'

'A round? 'What makes it a round?'

She sighed.

'The Siege Perilous ought to have given a clue. A ring is an unbroken line, it has no beginning and no end, the Round Table represented the brotherhood.'

'I suppose it was Merlin's idea,' I said.

'Nothing to do with Merlin. Other people have stumbled over the truth but few have recognised it. Arthur himself did. The brotherhood, he said, was the Christian God's will. By helping others we served Him,' the lady said.

She paused.

'I am a sorceress, a priestess of the old Gods worshipped in the stone rings that were made long before us by the people of Antiquity. I believe the Christians call us pagans,' she added impatiently. 'I am not a gentle soul, Matthew. We have had two failures with boys. Merlin is a weaver of dreams and very hard to rouse. He doesn't want to be roused for one thing, and it hurts his ancient bones for another.'

'I haven't got the tasks in my head,' I cried. 'All that talk about Merlin has muddled me. Why don't you rhyme it?'

'A rhyme? What is a rhyme?'

'A rhyme is poetry.'

'Like what?'

I looked about me.

'Look at that lovely tower
springing from the ground
like a very tall flower.'

'Never heard of such a thing,' Morgan said. 'Poetry is the music of the bards. Lofty sentiments and brave tales are passed on in beautiful language so we can learn from them.'

Then one of her ladies said the boy might be right. *Flower/tower* did stick in the mind.

'But rhyming is a new skill. What are you intended to become, Matthew?'

'A blacksmith's boy.'

'Pity it isn't a wordsmith. So, my ladies?'

> *'First follow your heart and make it sing.*
> *Then look for three signs that have to be 'other'*
> *to close the ring.*
> *Follow your heart and make it sing.*
> *Overcome sadness and Close The Ring.*

'Well done,' said Morgan. 'Now to the tasks.'

> *'The last knight, who was not, can be found*
> *on the flatlands' chalky ground.*
>
> *Do not turn back the dragon's breath*
> *Time and fire means certain death.*
>
> *To find the nobleman, who is not, Morgan will*
> *not give aid,*
> *But you Matthew, need not be afraid.*
>
> *The first knight, who was not, was feeling sorry*
> *Be careful or he will cause you worry_*

'Very good, my ladies,' said Morgan, 'I am most pleased. I will add that you, Matthew, must never lose the ribbon of time, without it you will be lost next time.'

What next time? I wondered.

'Repeat what my ladies have told you, Matthew, and hold the ribbon of time.'

The last knight, who was not, can be found
on the flatlands' chalky ground

` *Do not turn back the dragon's breath*
Time and fire means certain death.

To find the nobleman, who is not,Morgan will
not give aid,
But you Matthew, need not be afraid.

The first knight, who was not, was feeling sorry
*Be careful or he will cause you worry_*

I had got it right, I sighed with relief.

'But what is it all for?'

'When you have solved the riddle you will know all. The riddle will close the ring, for nothing can come of nothing,' Morgan said.

I had enough of knights who were, or who were not.

'You must ask the right questions to return to your village.'

Unless I asked the right questions, I knew I would be in Camelot forever. I wouldn't know what to do here and where to go and I would never see my home and my mother and Biddy and grandma and my father again. But what was it? And then, and just in time, I remembered something.

Chapter 6

I twisted the blue ribbon of time round and round in my hand, and then, and only just in time, I remembered the riddle of the Holy Grail. Percival had stood there like a dumb ox, but Sir Galahad had asked the right questions.

I would have to do the same, but what were they?

'How do I get back to my village?'

It must have been right, the colours were fading, and the lady's voice was getting fainter when she told me that next time it wouldn't be so easy.

`There are three signs, one of which has to confirm the other. And you have to find the answers without knowing the questions.'

'Really easy I don't think, how can you find an answer to a question you don't have?'

'You will recognise it if you use your brain,' she said, her voice now nothing but a sigh. 'And never lose the ribbon, without it you will be lost in time.'

'Even if I know the answers?'

'Just so,' the voice sighed.

The landscape before me dissolved into mere colours. When I turned round, there was a twisting path in front of me, but the lady's voice gave me heart; she wanted me to return to the village if I was to complete the tasks.

'Just so,' sighed the voice.

'Just so,' said my mother over her shoulder to Biddy. She was shaking me awake. 'We have overslept and we need wood for the fire.'

I stretched out as contented as a cat on a warm patch of ground now I was home and in my own bed.

'Why are you so clean? You went to bed covered in dirt from the journey. And just where did you find that blue ribbon?'

'It's the ribbon of time. I have been to Camelot and met a lady, she gave it to me. She said to tell you the Lady in the Lake was the Queen of the Fairies.'

'Queen of the Fairies indeed,' said Biddy, crossing herself. 'You have been in bed all night.'

Why did mention of the Fairy Queen frighten her? I thought.

When I gave Biddy the ribbon she looked at it, and then it happened; the ribbon floated towards me and into my pocket.

My mother crossed herself.

'Is it to do with the day of his birth?' she asked.

All Souls' Day, when the dead came back for one night.

'Aye,' said Biddy. 'I might burn some sage for the purifying and make him an infusion of St. John's Wort to calm him down.'

They had better take it themselves; they were more in need of it than I was.

Finally the fire was made up, we had breakfast, and my grandmother was dressed, sitting out the front step, catching a rare bit of sunshine. Sometimes she wandered off, but someone usually brought her back.

'Now, Matthew,' Biddy started to say, but she didn't get any further; the blacksmith's wife was heard out the front.

'Good morning mistress,' she shouted at grandmother. 'It's a fine day to watch the chickens scratching about in the dirt. Sometimes I wish I had nowt else to do.'

Inside, we all looked at each other. If we kept quiet perhaps she would go away, but no, the blacksmith's wife stood in the doorway blotting out the light.

'I was just conversing with the mistress about chickens. Do you lose many to the reynards?'

46

'Not many, one or two perhaps, they roost in the alders, but do come in,' said mother.

'I haven't come to talk about chickens,' she said, entering the cottage. 'I have come for the boy. You do recall the arrangements? When the boy is ten?'

'But I am twelve now because I was ill, so it doesn't count,' I said.

'What's a year here and there,' she said, and I was to fetch my things. She looked at me. 'He looks a bit of a milksop to me, if you don't mind me saying so. You can have him back when he is twenty-one, he won't look so clean then, I warrant.'

The lady in Avalon had also said my skin was as fair as a lily. I couldn't wait to grow a beard and bushy eyebrows.

'Get ready,' the woman said. 'I haven't got all day even if you have, you know what my girls are like.'

'As pretty as petals on a daisy,' said my mother.

`I will be with you this evening,' I said, 'there has to be enough wood to last until Sunday.'

'What makes you think you can skive off on a Sunday?'

'Because I am a free-born Englishman, that's why.'

'That's as maybe, but Himself has an order for a gate and he needs a boy most urgently. We also have a couple of pilgrims to put up, and you know what my girls are like.'

My mother said they were lovely girls, all of them, and what she wouldn't give for a clutch of girls - like the blacksmith's wife had - around her.

It softened the woman.

'Tonight will do nicely,' she said.

We watched her roll down to the village and out of sight. A sharp intake of breath made my mother and me turn round, and there, in the distance against a

47

watery blue sky, we espied my father talking to Thomas, the shepherd.

'That man could teach Lazarus how to come back,' said Biddy but I was pleased; my father was here to take over.

I ran up the hill to greet him. He held an animal in his arms, a black lamb, but as I got nearer I saw that it was a dog. It was Boy.

'He's in a right sorry state,' said my father. 'I had to free him from a trap. Let's take him home and see to him.'

The dog's ribs met his stomach he was so thin, his coat was mangy and one of his legs was bloody.

'Boy!' I cried.

He opened one sad brown eye and then the other, but he turned them towards my father. He lifted his head slowly and licked his face.

Boy had found a new master, I realised later when I took one last look around me.

The smoke curled around the fire and out of the smokehole the middle of the long room. My father, his dark hair falling over his forehead, washed the dog's injuries, helped by Biddy. My mother was spinning, her hand with the spindle raising and falling.

It all seemed very comfortable as I ran in the darkening afternoon. It wasn't only Boy, but also myself, who had found a new master.

**

Edwin's place

I paused.

Edwin, I had to remind myself, had his own life to lead. He had to go to school, eat with his family, and sometimes he played with some noisy boys. But he also made notes and listened to me carefully. And another thing, *living* and *telling* are about the same as a cat and a dog, not the same at all. *Living* can take days, weeks, and months. *Telling* can take a few hours in the evening and at weekends.

Now he looked at his notes, crossed out some words, and copied it all out onto a new page.

SACRIFICE

1) Your mother gave up her warm cottage and had this cough.
2) The Blessed Abbot renounced his wealth.
3) Mary under the cross gave up her son.
4) Sir Galahad fell down dead.
5 Your father left his cosy cottage to look for his lost son.
6) You had to go to the blacksmith.

THE TASKS AND THE RIDDLE SET BY MORGAN LE FEY

THE TASKS

The last knight, who was not, is to be found
on the flatlands' chalky ground.

Do not turn back the dragon's breath
Time and fire means certain death.

To find the nobleman, who is not,
Morgan will not give aid,
But you Matthew, need not be afraid.

The first knight, who was not, was feeling sorry
Be careful or he will cause you worry.

'Morgan le Fey can't help you, because she doesn't know about him,' he said.

'And why not?'

'Because he IS NOT. He is not dead, he is still alive, Matthew,' said Edwin. 'We'll have to hunt him down together. There's no school tomorrow, it's the summer holidays. Not *Holy Days*, just a few weeks off.'

'Do you know what the date is?'

'End of July,' Edwin said.

I was born on All Souls Day, when my parents thought I might not survive the first day of my life.

It was the day we honoured dead souls, I added.

'We don't do that now. We scare the daylights out of the living instead and call it Halloween.'

'I think that is the last day for me to complete my task and help my master.'

'The cut-off date?' asked Edwin.

What a good expression. It said it all, but Edwin remained hopeful. We had the holidays to solve it.

Edwin rose early the next day and I resolved to tell him about my time at the blacksmith in one day, without interruptions but with a few pauses for thought, but I had two listeners that day instead of one, much to Edwin's disgust.

'This is *for us two boys*, not for *grandmothers*,' he cried, but Edwin's grandmother, who had seen me clearly for a while, said she was *protecting* him; Edwin's parents would be worried if he talked to himself, or worse, laughed, *when they could only see him.* 'They would think you are crazy.'

Edwin told his grandmother, roughly, how I had come to be there.

She never turned a hair. I don't believe she was ever frightened of anything, I said.

'That's right,' she said. 'I don't have the imagination for it. But imagination is very overrated in my opinion.'

'Is there a princess in your story, Matthew?' she asked me. 'I always think a frog and a princess go together in a magical tale.'

'Grandma!' Edwin cried. 'Matthew isn't a 'story!'

'Carry on, Matthew,' she said, 'we haven't got all day.'

There were no princesses at the blacksmith's; however, I found a different kind of magic there.

It was the practical magic of the blacksmith who transformed crude iron into a shoe - fitting a horse's hoof precisely - with the aid of air, fire and water.

I didn't think of the blacksmith as a kind of magician when I ran through the village in the late afternoon to become his boy. I dreaded living with him in his house.

Chapter 7

Matthew

The blacksmith surprised me.

He was broad of forehead, and his reddish, curly hair crowned a regular-featured face sporting curly red mutton-chops. He was a giant of a man, but he seemed gentle. Could this really be the man who had threatened to burn my father's face off?

'You're here then,' he said when I stopped in front of the open forge where I watched the blacksmith and Eli, his man, moving in front of what appeared to be hellfire for some time.

'We can do with you, boy,' he said, wiping his hands on a leather apron.

He crossed himself. Then he spat.

'Did he have an accident, your last boy?' I asked.

'Only if you can call living to near sixty an accident. He died of living.'

There I stood, with my mouth open, wondering what to do when Matilda called out to me.

'You'll share a chamber with Eli. Just follow me for now,' she said. 'And stop gawking, you lot,' she added to her sisters crowding around her like chicks around a mother hen. 'Matthew is new here. How would you like it if you went somewhere strange and everybody stared at you?'

'It's only Matthew! He's not new or strange!' one of the girls said, pointing at me, 'so there. She thinks she is the master of everything, Matilda does,' she said, turning to me. 'I'm Abigail.'

Abigail had a head full of dark curls and two eyes which met each other on either side of her nose.

Apparently she wasn't cross-eyed until she fell

down the well, I learnt later, when she found herself upside down in the bucket.

Matilda had blue eyes, eyes as blue as the heart of the flame, eyes now burning vividly in her white face. Everything else was white, her lips, her eyebrows, her eyelashes.

'I've been baking,' she said. 'Just you wait until I take the loaves out from the oven at the manor. You'll be wondering why my face is so red.'

'At the manor? My mother uses hot stones around the fire for baking.'

'We'll we don't, so there, you know-it-all', said Abigail, 'and it's our turn for the oven today.'

'I must be off,' Matilda cried. 'We have guests. I put them in the stables for the night.'

I encountered two men with seashells - the sign of pilgrims - hanging from string around their necks as they hobbled out of the stables.

'We're on our way to the Shrine of St Edmunds,' they told me.

I knew that Edmund's head had been cut from his body by the Danes so his friends wouldn't recognise him after he was killed for not renouncing Christianity. But Edmund was found because his head, guarded by a wolf in the forest, kept calling out to them.

Heavily bearded and smelling unspeakably, the pilgrims had made a vow not to cut a hair on their bodies or wash themselves or their clothes until they reached their destination on foot.

Lodging the pilgrims in the stables now didn't seem such an uncharitable deed.

I sat well away from them in the evening. Grace had been said by one of them, the fat lard candles fixed on the wall giving a glow to the people seated around a long, wooden table.

There were the pilgrims, the blacksmith, his

wife, his man Eli, me and the girls. Matilda ladled out the potage, a thick, rich soup with chunks of lamb and bacon.

Everybody helped themselves to bread and cheese set out before them.

It was all so delicious, and I, who had expected to be in hell, now thought I was in heaven or that it was Christmas.

'Matilda, the ale, fetch the ale, girl,' the smith's wife cried, no sooner had the girl sat down. She got up, came back with a pewter jug, and sat down again.

'Help our guests, girl, fill their mugs,' her mother cried. 'Do I have to do everything?'

'That'll be the day,' Abigail muttered.

'What did you say?' demanded her mother.

'Abigail said "honour thy father and thy mother,"' Matilda cried.

The pilgrims smiled at her sweetly, and I, who had never spent an hour in the company of someone of my own age let alone a girl so full of life, was fascinated.

'Matthew is staring at Matilda,' Abigail whined. Then she screamed and said Matilda had kicked her under the table. She got up, danced around a bit and held one of her legs.

'Abigail fell down the well, and Matthew is our new apprentice,' said the blacksmith rising above it all. 'Tis his first day. He'll see to the fires in the forge.'

It was a long speech for the smith who was a man of few words, as I would discover.

One of the pilgrims opened his mouth and shoved some bread into it. In his hairy face it looked like a foxhole in the shrub.

'I'm from up North,' one of the pilgrims announced. 'I believe you still use charcoal in these here parts.'

The blacksmith was about to spit, thought better of it when he saw his wife looking at him, and nodded.

'Aye, boy, we do that, pine charcoal,' he said. 'Charcoal for intense heat. For the rest we use wood. Semi-hard and hard wood. Black Poplar like, or Elem and Hash. T'is an exact art for the boy to learn.'

'Elem and Hash? Oh, Elm and Ash. Up North we now use coal,' he announced. 'We dig it up out of the earth. Coal holds the heat about a hundred times longer than charcoal.'

'Never,' said Eli wringing his hands in awe.

I noticed his long, black mittens, reaching from his elbows to his knuckles.

'Easily ten times more,' the pilgrim said, revising his estimate.

'Where's that then? Where they dig it up?'

'Up North,' said the other pilgrim.

'I've always wanted to visit Upnorth if I knew where it was,' said Eli, helping himself to a chunk of bread.

Just as I wondered if I ought to tell Eli *up north* wasn't a village, the blacksmith's wife got up and pushed the bench back.

'Pots,' she cried.

The pilgrims and I looked at each other. Pots? Everybody bar the girls took off, and so did I. I groped my way out of the room and then followed Eli up narrow stairs, taking the turning to the right at the newel post, to our chamber.

The chamber was faintly lit by moonlight shining into a slit in the wall. I could just make out Eli's hostile movements. He was taking his belt off, swishing it in the air.

I ought to say something friendly, so I told him *up north* wasn't a village but a different part of the country, my father had visited it one time.

'Is that so?' he drawled.

It hadn't gone down too well, so I said how much I admired his black mittens. My mother wore mittens in the winter but hers frayed more easily.

'Mittens, boy?' cried Eli. 'Mittens? I'll give you mittens.'

I found myself grabbed by my neck and dragged downstairs by my hair. My bundle flew after me.

I sank to my knees and tried to think of a prayer. When none came to me I said, 'Well, Lord, you know how it is, Amen', and then spent an uncomfortable night in front of the parlour hearth.

As usual I woke early the next day and went outside where I found Matilda yawning in the yard. She pulled a pail of water from the well which tapped into an underground spring.

'I'll do that,' I said, taking the pail, emptying it into a backet, a large wooden through.

I yawned myself.

'Eli threw me downstairs, and all because I admired his black mittens,' I told her.

'Those are not mittens, silly,' she said. 'It's the way he washes. He only ever puts half his fingers into the water. You'll see for yourself shortly.'

Those mittens were dirt then, and right up to Eli's elbows, but how was I supposed to know?

'I'm glad you're here,' Matilda said, holding out her hands. 'It's wonderful to have somebody to laugh with. Abigail is just so miserable.'

I put my fingers into my mouth and gave a sharp whistle, then we both looked up to the sky.

'No pigs flying there, shepherd's boy,' she cried.

'Let's meet here before anyone else is up and about,' I said.

And that is what happened. I whistled for her early in the morning and we became friends. We even shared a name of sorts, I called her Mattie, and I had been called Mattie when I was little or ill.

But if I had made a friend, I had also made an enemy out of Eli.

Eli might be quiet and mind his business to all outward appearances, but Eli wasn't to be trifled with, as I already knew.

What I didn't know was that he would use a black cat and also my Aunt Biddy, who could make the lame walk and the dumb speak, to discredit me, but I would find that out shortly.

Chapter 8

Mattie and I flew apart when every member of the household stumbled into the yard, rubbing their eyes heavy from sleep.

'Yon pilgrim's in a bad way,' the blacksmith said, pointing to the stable. 'What do you reckon, mistress?'

'By All-The-Blessed-Saints, if you're not right,' his wife cried when one of the men crawled on all fours towards her and collapsed at her feet.

'Oh, I do hope he's not going to breathe his last breath under our roof.'

Eli lifted his hat.

'Right as rain last night, he was, all the way from Upnorth which ain't a village, and now look at him,' he drawled. 'I don't suppose that black cat yonder has owt to do with it? Ain't never seen a black cat round here afore. Not until that there boy turned up yesterday. Don't it mean bad luck or sumpten?'

'Don't be silly, Eli,' Mattie cried. ''Tis one from a batch of kittens we found in the stables last autumn.'

All eyes looked at the cat perching large, solid and black against a rosy dawn, peering into the chicken coop.

'The cat is only bad luck for the chickens,' I cried. 'Best shoo it off.'

'First bite to me,' Eli whispered to me, when at last the animal got off the fence to the households' combined cries of, 'Sshoo' and 'Getoutofhere', and then slithered out of the yard and towards the woods.

'Oh, I wish I was as light on my feet,' the pilgrim moaned. 'And to cap it all, we have by-passed Bury St. Edmunds.'

'Aye, we have that,' the other one sighed. 'We thought it was Clare until the smith told us otherwise.'

'Fetch mistress Elisabeth to help the poor soul, Matthew, now we are friends,' the blacksmith's wife cried, relieved that the pilgrim was not dying on her but merely had bad feet and a poor sense of direction.

Mistress Elisabeth was Biddy, Mattie reminded me. She fetched a pail and a milking stool and ran with me through the village, awaking to a new day.

I ran towards home, Mattie to milk the goats.

'Oh Matthew,' my mother sighed. 'Not in trouble already? Fetch your father, he's at the stream.'

'I don't need him, I need Biddy. One of the pilgrims is in a bad way. His feet have given up on him.'

'That I can cure,' Biddy said, reassuringly. 'I've come across the burning feet of martyrs before now,' she said.

'Likely he walked with a stone in his boots since he began his journey,' she said to the blacksmith's wife back at the smithy. 'I'll take it out and immerse his feet in cold and then hot water for a while. Then I'll bandage them. If only everything was as simple.'

Talking of simple, mistress,' the blacksmith's wife said later, 'I would be obliged if you could take a look at Poor Rosie.'

Poor Rosie was a dark, curly-haired girl of about four.

'Pretty as a daisy and as sweet-natured,' her mother cried, 'but she won't say a word. Never has done.'

'Open your mouth. Wide open now,' Biddy commanded.

Poor Rosie obeyed her.

'She's not deaf,' Biddy said, 'She might have been born tongue-tied but oftentimes it rights itself at about her age.'

Everybody looked at Poor Rosie to prove it.

'Say 'something,' the smith said.

'What? Something? she said.

She said it over and over again, her grey eyes wide open in surprise at the sound of her own voice.

All bar Eli were happy that Poor Rosie's speech had been unlocked.

'Mighty strange, boy,' he said later, watching the pilgrims walk out of our lives. 'First a black cat appears out of nowhere, and then your aunt makes the lame walk and causes the dumb to talk. Sinister, ain't it?'

'I am that too, so you best beware,' I cried, 'I have already transformed myself into a bad smell clinging to you,' but really I was afraid. The threat of the supernatural was almost impossible to fight. Especially for one who had crossed over.

'You really are stupid, Eli,' I added for good measure. 'I can't be both Matthew and a stink. I mean you stank long before I ever got to you.'

Chapter 9

'You and Eli arguing already? Blast the two of you to hell an' back,' said the blacksmith storming into the yard.

His temper was up with half the day gone and no work done. 'Time you were off to the log men, Eli. About ten days' sawing this time, I reckon. I want a couple of wagon loads for the boy to chop.'

'Eli has got his eye on Matilda and she's taken a liking to you,' he said after Eli had left.

'But he's far too old for you,' I said to her the next day when we met at dawn.

Mattie, at thirteen, was the eldest girl. The smithy would go to her unless there was a son and heir or cousins in the family.

'And pigs will fly if I don't make my own choice,' she cried, her flame-red hair flying about her face. But we both crossed ourselves. The unlikely had already happened, I had whistled for her.

It was late May, but for all I knew it could have been December, confined as I was to the smithy.

I worked well and hard every day, working the large bellows on the fire, holding a horse that didn't want to be shod, keeping the fire to the heat the blacksmith wanted; I aimed to find favour not only with the smith but also with Eli.

The danger laid with him.

He hadn't taken kindly to being told he stank, even if it was the truth.

I hardly ever went home, for most Sundays I chopped sawn logs to fill the ever-diminishing woodpile.

My hands started to blister and then they bled, looking like a piece of raw meat, but I wasn't going to give in. At first tears streamed down my face, then I grew used to the pain. I grew muscles in my arms and bigger shoulders, and my hands healed. I was so tired that I nearly nodded off most evenings at the dinner table.

I hardly managed to totter to the smithy to bank the fire for the night and then onto the large stable where I had made the first of the three indoor stalls my own sweet-smelling, cosy hide-away.

I had swept out the old dung, put an old horse blanket over bundles of straw and formed a pillow with hay.

Tonight, as always, I made sure the magic blue ribbon was in the bundle hidden under a bail of straw as I fell back on my resting place, when I hit my head on something hard and sharp.

I sat up, feeling the back of my head. My hand came away feeling sticky. It was blood from the sharpened axe, no doubt placed there by Eli who I espied standing in the darkening yard next to the chopping block, missing the axe buried there.

He was watching the stable.

I'll have him, so I will, I determined, or it will be the axe for my throat next.

I smeared some of the blood from my cut under my nose and stumbled into the yard.

'Bo-lo-od!' I screamed. 'Bo-lo-od. Mur-der!'

Then I fell to the ground.

'Are you my mother? I can't see properly,' I whispered pitifully.

Everybody was in the yard by now.

'Somebody put the sharpened axe where I lay my head,' I whispered, sitting up.

'T'weren't very sharp,' Eli cried. 'And why is there blood on his face and not ...' He stopped.'

'His head's cracked and his life's seeping away,'

Matilda cried. 'I best take him home.'

I tottered out of the yard leaning on her, tears in her eyes. Tears of laughter at my performance.

''I do have a headache. And a cut. And a bump, but I only meant to teach Eli a lesson,' I said.

'We've kept our part of the bargain. Matthew will not go back to the forge,' my father said later that night after he had seen to Eli. Whatever that was, I thought, although I realised Eli wouldn't take kindly to having two lessons.

'Give Matthew a week to recover, Eli and the boy are always playing tricks on each other,' I heard the blacksmith's wife say the next day.

'A nasty cut and bump,' Biddy said coming over, unwrapping my bandages, 'but he'll live.'

'It throbs when I lay down,' I said. 'I'll stretch my legs and go and see my father.'

Fat spring lambs dotted the newly greened hillside and inhaled the air fragrant with May blossom and cow-parsley.

I was drawn to the woods. I could do no other.

Twigs crackled underfoot as I ran up an incline where sunlight slanting through branches of a large oak was shaped like a star onto bluebells.

BLUE, LIKE THE RIBBON FLOATING TOWARDS ME AND INTO MY POCKET!

Someone had rustled round in my bundle at the stable. It could only be Eli.

The next night, my sleep was broken by a sharp whistle. When I sat up and got used to the faint light cast by the dying fire I saw that my father had gone again.

I heard the whistling again.

Matilda was whistling for me. Did she want to tell me something? Warn me about something?

Moving gently so as not to waken anybody I crept out, the dog close at my heels.

I sensed an evil presence so it couldn't be Matilda, but there was something or someone nearby. One of the tree trunks moved. When the tree trunk moved towards me, Boy took off, straight and silent as an arrow.

When I heard a scream, I took my courage into both hands and ran to the place where the tree trunk had moved, but - although nobody was there - I found a hammer on the ground.

Eli had meant to lure me out, and when he had, he would have set about me with the hammer. Had he used it on Boy?

I waited in vain for the dog. Where could he have got to?

Chapter 10

When I went into the cottage, I found the dog on my bed, resting his weary head between his out-stretched front paws. He opened his eyes, cocked his ears, and yawned.

'What were you doing outside all this time?' he seemed to ask, but it wasn't the dog, it was my mother who voiced the question.

'Looking for my father,' I lied.

'He'll be back soon,' she said, 'your father will be home now, he is no longer looking for the lost boy.'

'He's found him? So why isn't this boy here?

'The boy thought your father was crazy. "I already have a father", he said.'

'He told him to get lost, I suppose. That's what I would do,' I said, but my mother said he was most polite.

'Unlike some I could mention,' said Biddy.

My father wasn't here because he took him some clothes of my brothers, said my mother. 'You'll have to make do with what is left; this boy *is* your brother.'

Half-brother and most polite, but I had my doubts.

Who in the woods had meant to harm me? Was it Eli, or was it this mysterious boy my father had found?

But first I had to go back to explain things to Mattie.

'You're back then, boy,' the blacksmith said that afternoon at the forge. 'Don't hang about, there's work to be done.'

'I've come to tell you I'm not coming,' I said, feeling the blood rush to my face. It sounded stupid, which wasn't lost on Eli.

He sniggered.

He also limped heavily.

He'd been bitten by a dog, Mattie said.

So it was Eli.

'Ha. Ha. Ha,' I, who never learnt anything, said.

'Blast the two of you to hell an' back,' the blacksmith thundered, 'especially you, Eli, you're more than old enough to know better. I'll make a smith out of the boy yet. He's like a son to me.'

So I donned my leather apron and made up the fire.

'And no wimp either,' he added. 'I told your father about the state of your hands after the wood chopping and how you kept on without belly-aching.'

My ears pricked up. Last time round my father had thought I was too much like a girl.

'When did you see my father?'

'Never you mind,' the smith said shortly. 'Get on with it.'

'Son', smirked Eli after the smith was called away by a traveller.

'Don't make too much of me being like a son to the smith. I really don't need another father,' I told Eli. 'And I have returned your hammer.'

'I must have left it somewhere,' he said.

'Now you look like a boy what likes riddles,' Eli drawled. 'Am I right, boy?'

I nodded.

'What has four legs and flies?'

'An animal,' I suggested.

'What sort of an animal?'

'Any animal. I mean flies crowd around them,' I said.

'Not them sort. I mean an animal with four legs what can fly.'

I shook my head.

'T'is a cat with my boot up its backside,' Eli concluded triumphantly.

'That's not very good. A cat doesn't fly by itself.'

'Well, here's one 'specially for you. A better one. What has you and the fire got in common?'

'We both need feeding.'

'That's so, but that isn't it.'

'We both go out?'

'Nope,' Eli said. 'You have to breath to stay alive. You need air for living. Like the fire needs air for burning, you might say. See those hands? Big as shovels, ain't they?'

'They certainly are,' I cried. 'Wonderfully so.'

Eli pinched my nose lightly with one hand, holding the back of my neck in an iron grip with the other.

'About two minutes without air should do it. The boy died in his sleep, folk will reckon. And if a boy were foolish enough to sleep, he would be burned in the stable.'

And then he let go.

I didn't know what to do about Eli, but whatever my plan of action was, or wasn't, I would have to deal with Eli myself.

I thought of the lost boy, my brother. Maybe it would be good to have a brother who looked out for me.

We had a guest that evening, a brother in a white habit who sat next to me.

I didn't notice much else for all I could see at supper-time were Eli's enormous hands opposite to me, now folded in prayer.

'I would like to say the prayer tonight,' Eli said, casting down his eyes.

'God bless this food, and my master for providing the means for it, and our mistress for cooking it with Matilda's help.'

'And for Abigail who has also seen to the Brother's horse,' added Abigail.

The blacksmith said, 'Amen.'

'Amen,' said the mistress.

Eli coughed and said he had not finished.

'And Lord, look on me, a most miserable sinner, who has upset the boy. You know, Lord, I haven't meant any of it.'

'Amen. Poor Rosie and all the girls,' cried Poor Rosie.

'I HAVEN'T FINISHED!' Eli screamed, banging his fists on the table. 'And I repent, Amen,' he added quietly.

'Amen at last,' said Mattie. 'No use getting agitated, you will talk so slow, Eli. Nowt worse than a slow talker and a potage getting cold.'

Except perhaps Eli, who looked as mad as if he had stuck his face into a hornet's nest. Beneath the frown on his forehead, deep enough to split it into two, his narrowed eyes were small, green, unripe and poisonous berries.

The brother looked at the smith.

'Is there some trouble here?'

'Oh, aye, ahr,' the smith said. 'Some larking about betwixt Eli and the boy.'

'And the master's been like a dead horse in a ditch ever since it started,' the mistress cried.

'If you truly repent, well said, Eli,' the brother said. 'The Lord loveth a sinner who cometh to His righteousness.'

I turned my head slowly, unwilling to believe it.

'Brother Aloysius!'

'Ah, yes, t'is Matthew? I believe,' he said, as if he wouldn't know me if he fell over me. 'I've not heard that you're the new boy here. Is your family well? I haven't seen them yet.'

He was very tired and wished to be excused, he said, no need for a candle to light him to his chamber.

'A most acceptable repast, mistress, thank you kindly,' he added. 'And thank you, Abigail, for seeing to my horse.'

I had forgotten about Brother Aloysius's horse when I went to my bed at the stable.

It stood silent in the second indoor stall at the stable, his ears pricked forward. I stroked the horse, a soft-eyed brown cob, who watched me standing erect, as I paced the stable in the half-dark.

I felt bone-tired, but I didn't dare be a boy 'foolish enough to sleep,' as Eli had said.

I thought of hiding with the horse, but it might panic with a stranger so close to him.

If only the first stall I slept in could be locked from the inside, but the half-doors had a bolt on the outside to keep a horse in, and Eli could easily set the stalls on fire, I thought, when a familiar figure slipped into the stable.

A finger was placed over my lips before I could cry out.

'I had to be cool towards you, Matthew,' Brother Aloysius whispered. 'Eli might have smelled a rat. Your father came and fetched me and he asked me to see the situation for myself.'

'Is the blacksmith in on it?'

He was indeed, the brother whispered.

'The smith is unsure about Eli, but I'm not. Eli looked quite murderous when his blasphemy of a prayer was interrupted,' he said. 'Where do you sleep?'

'In the first stall.'

Brother Aloysius laid down on the blanket and rehearsed being Matthew, fast asleep.

I stood back. Would Eli be fooled by him under a horse blanket?

Not entirely. A full moon spread its light over the house and yard, faintly illuminating the stable. The brother's tonsure revealed the flesh-coloured top of his head.

He covered the glint with the blanket.

I patted the horse's head as I tip-toed to the third stall. I squatted on the floor, ready to spring up.

Now there was nothing to do but wait.

The silence filling the stable was different now, expectant, like the moment before darkness gives way to the dawn.

The smith would keep a vigil in the house. The trap was sprung, but would Eli be caught in it?

Chapter 11

The hairs on my neck rose and my heart was beating fast. I felt very frightened. Eli was now lurking outside somewhere, but he could move very silently in the dark.

I started to shiver and peered out, and then the traitor moon became my friend.

In the murky light I could make out Eli's figure. He was standing in the yard by the pile of logs waiting to be chopped, still as a tree, his hat pulled down to his eyes.

He moved to the stacked woodpile and looked in the direction of the stable.

'He's here,' I hissed.

'Get into the back of the third stall,' Brother Aloysius hissed back.

Not a minute too soon.

Eli appeared and then slid into the stable, just as I had moved silently into the last stall, peering out at him.

He stood in the entrance getting his bearings. As he looked into the first stall, the horse whinnied. He padded silently towards it, stroking his neck. When the horse quietened down, I edged to the back of the stall, pressing myself into the wall, praying my courage wouldn't desert me as I waited for Eli to peer into my hiding place.

Then I heard a soft rustling followed by a cry.

'Take that, you villain,' Brother Aloysius roared.

Sounds of a fierce struggle, and I leapt up.

The brother might have had the advantage of surprise, Eli had expected a boy, and not a grown man, but Eli cancelled this out through and years of hard, back-breaking work. He was as strong as the horse that was now getting alarmed, kicking the stall, throwing his head back and whinnying loudly.

When I lunged forward I saw that Eli had lost his hat in the struggle. He had forced the brother on his back, lifting his hand when I pounced. I pulled Eli off Brother Aloysius by his hair.

When Eli fell back I sat on him, pinning his arms back. He looked up at me, confused, and weakened by it.

Now I had him, I didn't know quite what to do with him.

I looked back at Brother Aloysius for guidance, but he was more concerned with freeing his legs, entangled in his habit.

Eli recovered his wits and wriggled free from my grasp like a snake and raised a knife. I fled into the yard followed by Eli and ran straight into the blacksmith who held me firmly with his strong arms.

'Let me go,' I screamed.

Then I ran into the stable where Brother Aloysius was calming his horse. He was rubbing him down and talking softly to him

We both stumbled out into the yard.

'If you didn't get hold of the wrong one, blacksmith,' Eli said, squatting like an evil toad on the roof above us. 'I'll spare you though. You're a good 'un, but I can't say it's been any kind of pleasure meeting the boy. It might be next time with this sharp knife.

'There won't be a next time. I SHALL GO HOME AND NEVER, EVER LEAVE MY COTTAGE AGAIN!'

I rubbed my tired eyes. When I looked up again, I saw there was no-one on the roof.

And then my father ran into the yard. He embraced me. 'Thank God you're safe,' he said to me. 'Eli has the devil in him,' he said turning to the brother and the smith. 'I grabbed him but he slashed my hand.'

His hand was pouring blood.

'I best let Biddy take care of it,' he said. 'Keep him safe, Smith, if you would be so kind, and I'll talk to you in the morning.'

'Bolt the door, I and let us have some light, mistress,' the blacksmith shouted once we were inside the house. He threw a log onto the embers in the parlour hearth.

'The cooper was knifed and Brother Aloysius was near-strangled out there.'

'Never had to bolt the door in living memory,' the mistress cried, lighting the candles on the wall and on the table.

And you go back to bed,' she shouted at the girls.

Brother Aloysius sunk into a chair at the table.

'It does my heart good just to look at these girls.

'It does that, and so does the mistress,' said their father after the girls went to bed. 'Once I leaned towards another. Lovely she was, young Elena, Matthew's mother, but then I wed the mistress, nowt to do with loveliness.'

'Oh?' said the mistress.

'The best thing for me. Then I hankered after a boy, but a boy appears to be more trouble than half-a-dozen girls put together.'

'Especially young Matthew,' said the brother. 'What persuaded you to tell that villain where you're to be found? He'll now lay in wait by your cottage.'

'But I won't be there,' I cried. 'I'll be off before dawn out of the village. Eli will be watching my cottage and the Sheriff and his men can nab him.'

When it was safe I would return, I said.

'You'll need some decent clothes in that case,'

the mistress cried. 'I have kept my menfolk's breeches and smocks for a boy of my own who I will never have now.'

She opened a chest and out came breeches and shirts, boots and a hat.

There was a loud knocking on the door.

'It's me, Father Peter,' said a loud, deep voice.

He was a black figure, thin-faced, who believed in suffering. He always put the fear of God into me in church and now it was no different.

He drew a deep breath.

'Eli came to my door,' he said accusingly. 'He wanted refuge from your persecution.'

'Don't interrupt, boy,' he thundered when I opened my mouth.

'When I turned my back, Eli struck me. When I came to, he had robbed me of all of my food. I came to find out what happened, Eli worked for you,' he said to the smith, while the mistress cleaned a nasty gash on his head.

Everybody bar the smith -who had used up a month's supply of words- had a tale to tell, and the priest left none the wiser. He threatened to return the next day, and we went to have our rest.

Oh, the pleasure of being safe just for the moment. I was lying next to Brother Aloysius in the guest-chamber, wearing some of my new clothes. I took the ribbon out of my pocket and put it with the rest of my new clothes in the bundle. When I looked down, the gap between my breeches and boots was gone; my clothes fitted me!

'There was bad blood between our families, but not now,' I said. 'So good can come out of bad.'

'Could you please stop fidgeting and let me get some sleep?' said the brother, 'but you're right, not all change is loss.'

'Just so, Matthew. Nothing can come out of nothing.' The soft voice was a whisper in the wind.

'What are you thinking?' Brother Aloysius asked after a while.

'Nothing can come of nothing.'

'Just so,' the brother said. 'Let us place ourselves into God's hands and pray.'

The next day, Mattie was downstairs preparing food for our journey.

'Father has gone to alert the men in the village to look out for Eli. Then he'll go into Bury St. Edmunds to fetch the Sheriff.'

Brother Aloysius saddled the horse and led it quietly out of the yard when a dark figure appeared in the yard; my father.

How upside down: he was staying and I was leaving.

'Off with you,' he said,' and keep your wits about you. I need to talk to Brother Aloysius now. In private.'

I bid my father goodbye and left him to talk to the brother.

Time was passing but it was still dark when we left the village. Our faces were struck by the air, cool and fresh, as we rode out of the village, with me seated behind the brother.

Mattie ran after us.

'You know what Thomas the shepherd will say, Matthew.'

'That boy will be harder to hold than a handful of bumblebees,' I said.

She laughed.

'Take care,' she said.

The horse changed from its gentle canter and broke into a trot as we left the village and headed towards a new and uncertain future.

Chapter 12

As the sun rose over the horizon, the horse fell back into a gentle canter, lulling me into a pleasant sleep.

I came to with a start, clutching Brother Aloysius's unbleached habit as I looked about me. Most villagers were distant black figures bent over fields, paying us scant regard.

The few we met on the path greeted the brother with pleasure.

I'd forgotten he dispensed healing in these parts. I had almost looked on him as our sole property.

'You got yourself another fine horse then, brother. What do you call him?'

'Blazes.'

'On account of his white forehead I warrant.'

'On account of how often I told him to go to blazes,' the brother said.

He smiled - I presumed sitting behind him- at the man running beside us, who grinned back, revealing a few solitary brown teeth like a broken-down fence.

'Her fever's gone down, Brother Aloysius, you'll be pleased to know. Come and see me soon. I have a tooth needs pulling.'

I advised the man to think twice about it.

Brother Aloysius had pulled out one of mine. I had clutched my torn and bleeding gum, whereupon he told me not to make such a darned fuss. If I felt pain and was still alive I 'should be thankful for it'.

'Who is this fine fellow?'

'Just a boy who doesn't know any better,' Brother Aloysius said.

I would have to learn to keep my mouth shut, I thought. This man would remember me if Eli came after us.

'And here we stop,' Brother Aloysius said.

'Already? Where are we?'

'Somewhere near Risby,' he said, dismounting.

I followed him.

A few flowers were wilting in a jar amongst the deep grass.

'I always say a prayer here,' he said. 'Maybe you can freshen up the flowers. There's a little stream yonder.'

It was not yet the season for the bright summer flowers, but I spotted some bluebells and primroses.

'Whose grave is it?' I asked. 'Was it somebody important?'

'Not in the scheme of things,' he said, 'and yet it is. Passers-by keep the grave fresh.'

It was a child who died there, he said, no more than three years old. He was taken ill with a disfiguring disease and thrown out of his cottage until he recovered. And he was found drowned on this very spot.

'Drowned? But there's no water here!'

'He fell face down and drowned in no more than a few inches of water laying there after a rainy season,' said Brother Aloysius.

'When Father Peter heard of the boy, he consecrated the ground and buried the boy with the Scared Rites and facing East. This grave is kept up for the boy, and in a way all children like him.'

He watched me putting the flowers on the grave.

'But now let's away,' he said when I had finished.

After a while I sensed Brother Aloysius had nodded off, probably because he wasn't answering my questions, and he was giving the horse free rein. We meandered past meadows and fields with grazing sheep or cows for some time.

The sun had reached its highest point when the horse stopped in front of a large and impenetrable thicket of hawthorn, awash with white May blossoms.

Hawthorn was the unluckiest plant in the world, doomed to represent the crown Jesus had worn on the cross. The sharp thorn slashing His forehead - the white blossom - turning into His drop of blood - autumn's red berry.

'Why have we stopped here? This is not a good place,' I said when I sensed the brother had woken up. 'Everybody avoids touching hawthorn. Even the birds.'

'Just so, and I really don't know how we ended up here,' Brother Aloysius said, coming to with a start. 'T'is rumoured the hawthorns guard the burial place of a Saxon knight.'

'*So his bones won't be taken away for all the world to see*,' I cried.

'No such thing, and I wish you wouldn't shout in my ear,' Brother Aloysius grumbled.

'Is he, who is buried here in the hawthorn, called *The Last Knight?*' I cried, jumping off the horse.

How did the rhyme go?

I took the ribbon out of my pocket.

Then it came to me.

The Last Knight, who was not, can be found in the flatlands' chalky ground.

'Are we in the flatlands? And is this chalky ground?' I asked.

'I suppose so,' the brother said slowly.

He shook his head.

'For a minute I thought that brown ribbon of yours flashed bright blue. No more than an odd trick of the light, I expect.'

He held his hand out.

'Up you get. I don't like this place.'

I jumped up and we rode off, my heart light as a feather.

Easy, I thought. One task already completed. Now to the next; the dragon's breath. Or might it be about finding the last knight who was not the last knight, I wondered, riding along as Brother Aloysius was telling me a bit about Sir William Saxmund of Exning.

'Who is he?'

'Questions, questions. I just told you. Oh, I see what you mean. Your father told me to take you to his estate in Exning. He wants to know where you can be found when it's safe for you to go home.'

He paused.

'It's a good plan. We grew up together, Sir William and I.'

I thought about it.

'What would I have to do at the hall?'

'You might become a pot boy or a stable lad, or even a companion to Sir William's son, Jacob.'

'How old is Jacob?'

'Thirteen, or thereabouts,' the brother said.

William Saxmund and Aloysius Fairbrother, as Brother Aloysius was called when young, had been childhood friends. They fought each other to be the best in archery, languages, education, hunting.

They both fell in love with the fair Isabel, who couldn't make up her mind between her two suitors.

I was disappointed to hear it.

'I always thought you loved *my mother* when you said you were crossed in love.'

'Not at all, although young Elena was a sweet, most lovely maid.'

William and Aloysius both went on a pilgrimage to the Holy Land while the fair Isabel, who was very young, grew up and decided who she missed the most.

'And it wasn't you,' I said.

He sighed and continued.

They were waylaid by a band of robbers but they fought well, although William broke his leg in the scuffle.

'The bone was set by a Saracen, a most marvellous healer,' Brother Aloysius said.

'Did you convert him to Christianity?'

'He held most strongly to his own religion,' said the brother, 'but he was a marvellous healer, as I said, and Sir William walks without the slightest of limps. That's what makes it so sad.'

I didn't dare ask why this was sad, although I was dying to.

While William Saxmund was away his father died, William's younger brother ensured there would be little left of the inheritance. He turned into a wastrel and spendthrift. As the fields turned to weeds and the cattle left untended, the estate and the hall fell apart in the span of a few years.

'And he repented and became the Blessed Abbot in Clare,' I cried.

'Just so. And stop shouting into my ear.'

William gathered his serfs and made them into tenants and paid-servants and restored the land. Then he rebuilt the hall which had fallen into disrepair and he married the fair Isabel.

King Edward knighted him when he heard of his endeavours in the Holy Land.

'Edward wants to create another Camelot,' the brother said. 'The knights will have to fight for him in return for the king's favour. He's even built a Round

Table.'

'Out of Wood?'

'What else?' said the brother.

'The Round Table was made out of the knights' shields slotted together, but it wasn't really round, the place of the Siege Perilous was empty.'

Brother Aloysius laughed.

'I expect your mother told you the Arthurian Tales she heard when she was a nursemaid in Clare.'

'Morgan le Fey might have told me, if I met her,' I said.

'Or not, you strange child. Anyway, King Edward gave William hunting rights in all of his forests.'

William, now Sir William of Exning, was well set up, whereas Aloysius's mind turned towards healing and peace. He joined the Austin Friars when he took the tonsure.

'And it does suit your round face so marvellously well,' I cried.

He laughed.

'Time to break bread, I think, and let us see what the fair Matilda has prepared for us. There's good grazing here for the horse.'

We dismounted, sitting on a grassy knoll, eating in silence. At least I was. The fair Matilda! How about that! I couldn't wait to tell her and thank her for the bread, cheese, bacon and two honey cakes she had wrapped up in a cloth.

Brother Aloysius wrapped his food up, perhaps he wasn't hungry, or perhaps he was saving it for somebody else, I thought when I heard his stomach rumbling.

'Can you tell what it means when somebody says "make you heart sing"?'

'I have absolutely no idea,' he said. 'Who said

it?'

'I have absolutely no idea,' I lied. 'I'll make my own way to Sir William Hall,' I added before he called me an odd child. 'Just point me in the right direction.

'It would be a blessing,' the brother said. 'I have a mind to see another child. Take a shortcut through the forest. Follow the bridlepath for an hour and then turn onto the footpath leading to the left.'

'I suppose you can tell the passing of time by the sun and the rumbling of your stomach, and do clear your mind of ancient tales,' he added. 'Take your bearings from the sun. You'll see the house and paddocks and barns from there.'

Brother Aloysius blessed me and urged me to keep a stout heart. I picked up my bundle and set off towards the woods.

Then I turned round.

'Which left?' I shouted, but Brother Aloysius was already out of sight.

I could never tell my left from my right, but I ran on and I never looked back. I had developed an aversion to it. I ran on until I was swallowed up by the trees.

Chapter 13

I soon found the bridlepath leading into the woods.

It was muddy, churned up by horses' hooves, so I cut myself a stout stick as I wanted to make good time.

I also aimed to make a good impression when I presented myself at the hall, so I tucked my breeches into my stockings. My new clothes still gave me great pleasure. My arms no longer stuck out of the jacket-sleeves like a scarecrow's, but I would have to take care not to look too tidy for a pot boy, I thought, pulling my boots from the mud with squelching heaves like that time when I had accompanied my mother to Clare. It seemed so long ago, I thought, and so much had happened since.

I might have grown up a bit, for I could not have done this journey on my own then.

I thought of the blacksmith and his wife and Mattie and of all the people I had met, and of their great kindness. I also felt very pleased with myself for completing the first task set by Morgan le Fey, although- worryingly- I had not felt any great joy about the *Last Knight*.

I trudged along, congratulating myself on my newly acquired maturity, when I stopped. I had been walking for some time, surely more than an hour, and I had seen no path turning to the left whichever side that might be, but I knew the sun sank in the West.

West was opposite to the East. South was at noon, at the sun's highest point, and North was at night.

When I looked about me I saw that the woods had changed. Wide-apart oaks through which riders could hunt the hart were replaced by more closely massed trees. The greenery underfoot of creeping ivy giving way to unfurling fronds of ferns were replaced by last year's dead leaves and old beechnuts, crunching underfoot.

I walked very fast but I was getting ever deeper into the forest that was darkening now for the trees were very dense, almost forming a green roof.

When I had last looked up into the sky, the sun had been at its highest point. But now the sky was obscured by heavy, dirty grey clouds. The light began to fade, when to my joy I spotted a small path turning away from me.

I walked along until I stumbled over a root as thick as a man's arm.

I picked myself up and looked at the path. It hadn't been beaten out by men but by deer. Beeches wore long green skirts, ending where the deer could no longer reach their tender leaves.

I came across one then, a pretty fallow deer, startled into stillness bar its twitching black, velvety nose, and then the path stopped.

Four red fox cubs played near a foxhole, pouncing on each other, their ears large and sharply pointed, but they suddenly disappeared. I wished I could when I heard an animal crashing through the greenery.

A wild pig!

Always face a charging pig and never run away, my father had said, 'hit it on the nose with a stick and then chase it off.' But would it keep still, I thought as hid behind a tree?

It turned and got ready to charge again, when it changed its mind and disappeared into the undergrowth.

I sat heavily on a fallen log, when the rain started to fall in great drops, drumming heavy on leaves. My legs gave way now that one danger was over and new ones threatened.

Was that rustling noise a whole herd of wild

pigs?

And then I heard the long, drawn-out howl of a wolf in the far, far distance.

I tried to get up, but when I panicked I always felt it in my knees, as if my heart had dissolved and was lodged there and I couldn't move.

I didn't know where I was. I would be late. Another pot boy would turn up at the hall.

It was raining heavily now and night would fall. Although I was unable to see the North Star, the Pole Star, I knew lichen grew on the trees' North side, but, alas, I was too panicky to use this information.

I had to move to keep my panic at bay, so I forced myself to stand up.

'I am Matthew, the cooper's son,' I cried to give myself some courage.

'Who?' a voice above me asked politely.

'Matthew, the cooper's son from Horringer, if you please,' I stammered.

'Who? Who?'

I peered up into the tree where I saw two black eyes in a wise, white face, placed on a head that swivelled right round.

'Who? Who? Who?'

The owl's cries mocked and pursued me as I fought my way through dense trees, their branches snapping and rebounding on my face.

I stopped and remembered what my father had told me.

'Stretch your arms out as wide as you can. That is the span we can see,' he'd said.

I stretched out my arms, and suddenly I was able to see a path where I walked on, more hopeful of reaching the edge of the wood.

Instead I found a small log cabin sitting squat in a wide clearing.

Maybe it was a charcoal burner's hut, maybe it was used by hunters, I thought as I went in. There were a few furs on the ground, bundles of faggots.

In the middle was a small brazier, next to it a pair of saddlebags.

I threw a log onto the glowing embers before I investigated the saddlebags crammed with two loaves and some cheeses and smoked bacon.

I sat down and warmed my hands.

Warmth, what more could I want? Bread and cheese, maybe, but not until it was offered to me by someone, but what I was most urgently in need of was to KEEP MY WITS ABOUT ME.

This wasn't an inn welcoming the weary traveller, so was I completely crazy? Didn't this look like a hide-away? A hide-away for someone up to no good?

I hastily cut off some bread and cheese and stuffed them in my bundle, I did not want to starve to death in these woods, when I heard a noise. Someone was crashing through the undergrowth in my direction.

I didn't linger.

Grabbing my bundle I sped off.

For a moment I thought of hiding behind the hut, but the only real hiding place seemed to be an old oak tree at the edge of the clearing.

I tied my bundle around my neck with shaking hands and climbed its branches as far as I dared. The leaves had not fully unfurled, but I stopped when the branches became thinner and couldn't support my weight.

Nevertheless, I was high above Eli, for it was he who came crashing into the clearing.

'What the...' he said, staring at the open hut. 'I'm sure I let that there fire go out.'

He disappeared for a minute.

When he came back, he brandished a burning piece of wood. He walked around the hut several times before he was satisfied no-one was lurking in the immediate neighbourhood.

'Poachers, eh,' he said. 'I'll give 'em poachers. Disturbing my hut.'

I breathed a sigh of relief. I was safe for the moment, sitting securely in the tree's gable. What's more, I knew of Eli's whereabouts which was all well and good. What if Eli looked up in the light of the next day and saw me? Should I take off now?

I sat there in an agony of indecision. Perhaps nobody ever looked up.

I was getting tired and hungry and wondered how Eli was here; he had walked, and not ridden - like me- on a horse. Perhaps he knew a short cut, and perhaps he had overheard my father telling the brother where to head for.

I suddenly came to.

Below me all hell had broken loose between Eli and what looked like a poacher with a couple of dead rabbits slung over his shoulders.

They faced each other like warring dogs.

'*My hut*, has been for all time,' the poacher said, fists up.

'T'ain't.'

'You're up to no good.'

'And I s'pose you are,' Eli said, going for the man with his flaming torch. The poacher knew when he was beaten and disappeared silently.

I sniffed.

I thought I could smell burning.

When I looked down, Eli came running out of the hut, saddlebags slung over his shoulders.

He was packed up, ready to leave in a hurry. He looked about him one last time before he scurried away, in the opposite direction to me.

And then the cabin went slowly up in flames.

Chapter 14

I didn't watch the crackling flames for too long although I realised the oak was out of their reach. I was more concerned with getting away from Eli.

I climbed down and dithered by the clearing.

I should make a move, but the light and warmth from the fire was tempting, when I thought I heard what sounded like a child who was crying.

I followed the sound and nearly fell over the boy I saw by the faint light of the burning hut. He was sitting in a tree-root, crying into his arms.

I shuffled my feet and coughed.

He looked up and wiped his eyes.

'Who are you?'

'I am Matthew, the cooper's son. Who are you?'

'Don't you know?'

'No, but I don't know many people, I wouldn't recognise you if you were as famous as the Bishop of Bury St. Edmunds and I could see you clearly.'

'I don't know many people either,' he said. 'They won't let me.'

He was shivering in the tunic and breeches he wore.

'I'm wearing deerskin,' he said. 'The best. It has to be. I am Jacob.'

'Sir William Saxmund's son?'

He nodded.

'I ran away. Can you help me up and hand me my crutches?'

'Crutches?' I said. 'You ran away into THIS FOREST on crutches? That was very brave of you. I couldn't have done it.'

'Really? Couldn't you?'

When Jacob stood up, supported by his crutches, I could see his right leg was about ten inches

90

shorter than the other, but what struck me most were his shoulders.

'You have the most marvellously strong shoulders I ever saw,' I said admiringly.

He started crying again.

'That's the nicest thing anybody ever said to me. Everybody tries to say nice things to me. They tell me I have a pretty face, but it's not the same thing at all,' he sniffed.

I hadn't liked being called a pretty boy by Morgan le Fey when I had crossed over.

'I know how you feel,' I said.

'No, you don't. You're just an ordinary, rough village boy. What is your name?'

'Matthew.'

'I'm hungry. Have you brought me anything to eat?'

I pointed out nobody knew where he was because he had run away, so nobody could bring him anything to eat, but he could share what I had.

We were by then sitting at the edge of the clearing, warming ourselves and eating Eli's bread and cheese.

'I was running away from the noise, Matthew,' Jacob said after a while.

'The noise?'

'I make a noise when I walk around at home. Well, my crutches do. Click, click, click, click. Everybody knows here comes Jacob the cripple.'

'This bread and cheese is most excellent fare,' he added into the silence only broken by the crackling fire.

'Sometimes I wish I was dead. When we're dead *we'll all be made alike*. It says so in the Bible. My priest told me.'

'You have your own priest?'

He nodded.

'He's very learned. He rides over once a month from Exning to hear our confession. Do you go to church?

'Four times a year mostly, Christmas, Good Friday, Easter and Ascension Day.'

'That wouldn't do for me.'

Well, he had his own priest, but I would rather have Brother Aloysius, I thought.

'If we're all *made alike,* and it's the first I've heard of it, how about if we're all made into Jacobs?'

He started to laugh.

'Can you imagine the noise, everybody click-click-clicking along?'

He told me he had made his escape by crawling along the gallery of the hall and down the stairs. He had a spare pair of crutches and he had set off.

'It wasn't easy. The doors are enormous, and so is the key. I could hardly turn it. Pulling the crutches out of the ground was also difficult, but it was very silent. That was the nice part. Nobody could hear me. I made off into the woods, and that was fiendish, all those branches and tree roots.'

He had become too tired and too cold to walk.

He had rested and fallen asleep and then a man trod on him, and he realised he could never be like anybody else and enjoy the countryside.

'Nobody enjoys the countryside at night.'

'Oh? Don't they? I would like to ride, but will they let me?'

'You could have special stirrups,' I said. Then I recalled Morgan le Fey and the ladies. 'Or you could ride sideways, like ladies do, if your leg hurts.'

'It doesn't and I could, always supposing I survive the night. And they wouldn't let me ride.'

It was being so cheerful that kept him going, I

said.

'Not as a general rule,' he said, and we laughed again.

'What brings you here, Matthew?'

I told him about Eli who was after marrying Mattie when she was of age so he could have the smithy, and that he was trying to kill me when Mattie and I took a liking to each other.

'Is she your sweetheart?'

'I don't know. It's just...that we belong to each other, I suppose. Always will. When I was little or ill, I was called Mattie, and sometimes she is also called Mattie. We even share a name.' '

'That'll never happen to me. I don't know any girls who are named Jacob,' he said. 'But Eli won't come back. He tried to kill you first, and then he committed arson here. They'll soon catch him.'

We agreed it would get worse for Eli as it got better for me.

Jacob began to shiver desperately in spite of the heat the burning hut gave off.

'We could lie down together with our arms around each other and cuddle each other to keep warm,' I said. 'We all do that at home in the worst of the cold winter.'

'KEEP EACH OTHER WARM? CUDDLE UP TO YOU? I think not, village boy. You had better give me your coat.'

I took my coat off and wrapped it around him.

The blue veins on his hands stood up like small branches, and I was getting worried. I ought to fetch help, but where was help to be found?

'If I die in the night you will get the blame,' Jacob said, and on that cheerful note we fell asleep.

Chapter 15

It was still dark when I woke up cold to my bones.

The cabin was now a smouldering grey mass before us. I checked Jacob. He was still alive judging by his grumbling about being cold and stiff.

I told him he was a worse grumbler than Biddy.

'Who is Biddy?'

'My aunt.'

'Oh,' he said, as we set off towards the edge of the forest, guided by the light of the approaching morning. 'I might be a grumbler, but you are very bossy. Nobody dares bossing me about as a general rule.'

He was prevented from doing all sorts of things he wanted to do. He was very rarely allowed to venture outside. He wasn't allowed to ride. They might put it to him very nicely, but it came to the same thing, I told him; *he was bossed about*.

He had never thought of that, he said, swinging painfully slowly through the trees, stiff in every limb.

We finally reached the edge of the forest.

A girl with her back to us was milking goats.

'Mattie,' I cried.

'Wrong girl. I'm Rachel,' she said. 'Are you Matthew? The pot boy from the hall?'

'How do you know?'

'My sister Martha works there and she came looking for you in case you got lost. But what on earth are you doing here? You should have got there last night.'

'You're a pot boy at the hall, Matthew? How splendid. But we better keep our friendship a secret, otherwise they won't let us meet,' Jacob, ever hopeful, said behind me.

'Are you Jacob from the big house?' Rachel

asked. 'Only if you are, there'll be hell, ab-so-lute- hell, to pay. The whole countryside is alive, riders are looking for you.'

'Why?'

'They think you've been kidnapped and held to ransom.'

As if to underline the point, the silhouette of a rider appeared, dark and threatening against the pink early light of the day.

We could see him more clearly now as he rode towards us, fast and furious.

'I don't want to go home just yet,' Jacob cried. 'Let's hide.'

'Are you sure?' I asked, but as he was already amongst the trees, Rachel and I followed him.

'Why am I hiding?' Rachel asked as the rider thundered past us.

'Keeping up with me,' Jacob said. 'Ha! Normally it's the other way round. You must be a magic boy.'

I held up my hand to quieten him, I thought I heard a faint rustling of leaves behind me, but I dismissed it as a deer.

When the rider returned, we waited to see him disappear from view before we came out of the trees.

'Bother these things,' Jacob said. 'Let me have your stick, Matthew.'

When he threw his crutches to the ground and walked leaning on the stick, Rachel said we had four good legs between us all.

'Four?'

'With the stick. I was never any good at counting,' she said.

'And I'm not good at directions,' I said. 'I wasn't sure which left to take.'

I held out my hands.

'This left, or this left?'

'That left is your right,' said Rachel. 'Look, you have a small mole on your right hand, you can go by that until you get used to it.'

As easy as that!

'What does a pot boy do exactly?'

Rachel said a pot boy did all the chores in the kitchen nobody else fancied doing

'So I'll be the lowest of the low, like Percival at the court of Camelot,' I said.

'Oh, you know these stories?' Jacob cried. 'Well, it hasn't done Percival any harm.'

Jacob didn't look on the bright side of life as a general rule, I told Rachel as we sat on the knell as day broke, sure in the knowledge somebody would come for Jacob shortly.

'You've lost your hat in the woods, Matthew,' Rachel said.

I felt my head.

'So I have.'

'And your jacket.'

'Jacob's got it. He said if he died of the cold I would get the blame.'

Rachel laughed, and after a while Jacob and I joined in.

'So, Jacob,' a deep voice behind us said. 'Are you enjoying yourself? I hope you do realise your mother fell down in a swoon and has taken to her bed when we found you'd gone missing.'

We turned round.

That was my first sight of Sir William.

He was tall. He had piercing blue eyes in a broad, handsome face with a neatly trimmed blond beard. He wore a hat from under which his red-gold hair streamed behind him.

I helped Jacob to his feet.

'I have had the best time of my life, Father,' he said. 'I wasn't kidnapped. I didn't want to spoil things for you, I just ran away from the noise of my crutches.'

Something crumpled in Sir William's face.

Then he shook his head and strode towards us, scooping the boy up in his arms.

'Just lend me your arm, father,' he said. 'I walked quite well leaning on Matthew's stick. I met him in the night. He got lost when he couldn't follow Brother Aloysius's directions. He didn't know which left to take.'

'I didn't know there were two,' Sir William said. 'So, Brother Aloysius,' he added. 'And how is he?'

The question took me by surprise.

'He always asks after our health,' I said. 'I never thought he had a health of his own.'

'To inquire about,' I added.

Sir William looked at me, his head cocked on one side like an inquisitive sparrow.

Then he laughed.

'I'll have to tell him he is a god-like being when I see him, but perhaps he knows that already. Now show me where Jacob's crutches are, if you would be so kind. Matthew, isn't it?'

I nodded.

'And what is the name of the fair girl?'

'T'is Rachel, sir,' she said.

'I knew her name wouldn't be Jacob,' Jacob said glumly.

Sir William called him 'an odd child' as he rode away with him to the woods where we had left Jacob's crutches. Rachel and I ran after them. The goats were still tethered there, looking malevolent with their knowing eyes and pointed beards and cloven hooves, but the crutches were gone.

'Most odd,' said Sir William, 'most odd. So.

97

Who would want to steal a pair of crutches?'

Eli would, I thought, he would come back like a bad cough. He would enjoy tormenting a crippled child. I wouldn't put anything past him, even kidnapping Jacob.

I would have to warn Sir William, but would I see him again? I thought as he and Jacob rode off.

I bid Rachel goodbye.

Then I ran on in the direction Sir William's horse had taken, but the hall couldn't be missed.

It sat square, majestic, in the middle of the green grass of Suffolk's flatlands, closely flanked by dark pines and surrounded by barns and outhouses. Like the castle in Clare, it had an impressive stone front with enormous oak double-doors.

Many mullioned windows - as my mother had called them - twinkled from the large number of chambers of the second floor.

I made my way to the back of the house to the kitchen as befitted a pot boy, the lowest in the pecking order.

I felt sorry for myself cowering by the threshold. Jacob and Rachel both belonged to families who looked out for them every day, but I was alone.

I was overcome with a sudden longing to look on my village, enter our cottage, see my mother smile at me, walk to the smithy and whistle for Mattie.

I was sick to death of getting to know new people and put names to their faces. I was sick to death of having to fit in, but there was also Eli, a danger hovering in the distance.

I made a bargain with myself; if no-one opened the door I would turn back and go home.

So I got up and knocked on the door. Quietly, hesitantly. When my quiet knocking turned into an enormous noise, I knew who was behind it. I looked at the ribbon and I wasn't surprised that it had turned blue.

'I'is Morgan le Fey,' I cried just as the door was flung wide open.

'No, I'm not. I'm Martha,' a girl with a pleasant face said, 'I'm Rachel's sister. Come in.'

Chapter 16

'Come in. Don't just stand there with your mouth wide open. You're not here to catch flies,' Martha added. Her white cap was rammed down to her eyes. 'You're the new pot boy, it is to be hoped.'

I could not deny it as I went past the storeroom and into the kitchen housed in a separate building running alongside of the hall, divided by a passage.

The kitchen had been hidden by the pines when I had looked at it from a distance. It was a huge long and hot room, full of activity centred on a long hearth heating up many large black pots on trivets.

'Such a to-do, we have company tonight,' Martha cried, wiping the sweat running down her round face with her apron. 'Elsie! Stop turning! Get up. The pot boy is here at last.'

She turned to me.

'Put an apron over those good clothes of yours and sit over there with Frog and turn.'

'Certainly,' I said. Frog? Turn?

She pointed to the large chimney place with two seats on either end. One was empty. The other was occupied by a boy who was turning the handle on a spit with some difficulty, due to the weight of a very large pig roasting over a fire.

I assumed it was a pig, for its head and feet and tail were missing.

'Boar,' said the boy I sat down opposite to, and then we turned the handles on either side rotating the spit.

'Was it wild?'

'Not very pleased,' he said. 'You're the first one who hasn't heard it,' he added when I laughed. 'They make brawn and things out of the head and trotters. I'll show you.'

We left the boar and went into a chamber adjoining the kitchen.

'See?'

Platters of brawn decorated with bay leaves, platters of cold meat pies without their crusts surrounded by apples, apple-pies with their crusts on, honey cakes, and platters of red and yellow...

'Jellies,' said Martha rushing in. 'They use saffron for the yellow and claret for the red. Now get on with your turning. Cook is spitting blood.'

'Are you Frog?' I asked the boy when we were turning the spit once more.

'That's right.'

'Why are you called Frog?'

'Because I look like one.'

His head sat on his squat body with very little neck. He had a square face with skin like bark, and his cheeks wobbled every time the boar did when we turned it, which was every minute.

'Don't you mind?'

'Nah,' he said. 'Now if it were Toad, that'd be a different story. One of my brothers had a dead one around his neck when he got a poisonous ague.'

'Did it cure him?'

'Not really, he died, but it might have done. Like cures like. Toads are poisonous, but frogs ain't.'

'You must be Matthew,' he added. 'We were expecting you yesterday.'

'Aye,' I said, too tired to go into it. I kept on turning, trying not to inhale the delicious aroma of the slowly cooking boar.

I nearly dropped off to sleep around noon when a girl brought us bowls of hot potage. We stopped turning.

"No salt on this,' said Frog. 'We have salt in the evening. It comes in grey grains and is very expensive.'

My mother salted down beef, so I knew about it.

What I didn't know was that every servant and guest dined with Sir William and his family in the great hall.

I would see Jacob again, and I might even have a chance to voice my fears over Eli.

Or not.

This wasn't exactly the blacksmith's household. Sir William had untold servants swarming around him like bees around a hive.

'Salt goes lumpy when it gets damp,' Frog explained, 'so they sit above it. Servants sit below it, and you and me are the most below you can get.'

'Exciting life, ain't it,' he said when we changed over to use our other arms. 'I used to be a logger myself. Used to fresh air and woods. Being cooped up drove me nearly mad at first.'

He looked at me critically.

'I expect you're not used to hard work with your lily-white skin.'

'Call this hard work? Nothing to it. I used to be a blacksmith's boy.'

I showed him my calloused hands and then pulled a face at him. He stuck his tongue out, and for the rest of the afternoon we pulled faces at each other.

'It's a contest. They're pulling faces and Frog's the winner,' a girl's voice said.

A small girl of about three was talking to a slightly taller one.

She was pointing at Frog.

'He was born like he is so it doesn't count,' the taller girl said.

'Martha!' Frog shouted. 'Get them there maids away afore the boar spits on them.'

'It's dead, so it can't spit,' the taller girl said.

'But a dead pig smells better than a live one.'

'Whatever are those maids up to now,' Martha cried, running over, wiping her hands on her apron. 'I ain't really got time to take them across,' she added, taking hold of their hands. 'I haven't made the crust for tomorrow's meat pies yet. That's how it is, Matthew. Tis Jacob this and Jacob that and Jacob the other. The nursemaid lets his sisters run wild, the little lovelies.'

'How about their mother? Doesn't she care?' I asked.

'Lady Isabel is not well. I'm told she oftentimes suffers from a heaviness of the soul,' Martha said. 'I sometimes think that's my trouble except I haven't the time for it.'

We watched her as she took the girls away.

In the heat and steam of the kitchen they seemed out of place in their white dresses, their long fair hair bouncing on their backs with each determined step.

'Martha would make a champion nursemaid, she can't get enough of the little maids' company,' Frog said.

'Why isn't she?'

'Pecking order, see. I myself aim to be a stable boy next. Get out into the fresh air once more.'

He stared into the distance, and all of a sudden he cried; 'Stop! Done.'

The boar had turned from golden to brown. We got up and stretched ourselves before we crossed the passage between kitchen and hall, where we placed burning torches in holders on the walls of the ante-chamber and eating hall.

Fires were already burning brightly in wonderfully big braziers, throwing dancing shadows onto the walls. Maids scurried in with the food I had seen earlier, setting the longest table I had ever seen with pewter plates, spoons and knives.

Silver goblets sat at the top table facing the long table, in the middle of it was an enormous bowl called a wassailing bowl filled with cider, Frog said, and   tankards around it..

'Spiced cider for us. Wine for Sir William and his guests. It comes from the port, so do the grapes,' Frog said. 'They have walnuts and apples and grapes for a finish. Best go back and wash our hands before we start cutting the bread.

He laughed.

'Brown is brown wherever it comes from,' he added, 'but they're particular like that.'

We cut the top off from untold round loaves, setting the upper crusts out in rings on platters for the top of the table, the dark underside for the servants and tenants.

I followed Frog's lead and removed my apron, and then we attached ourselves to a line of men and boys coming into the kitchen. They wore tidy clothes and bright kerchiefs and chatted excitedly as they filed into the dining-hall and stood by their places.

The cook placed a custard for the little maids on the top table before she and her helpers came among us.

Sir William and his guests came down the stairs from the gallery leading into the ante-chamber and then into the hall. We sat down when they were seated, and it was the Stewart, Frog whispered, who brought in the boar's head - an apple stuck into its mouth, bay-leaves into its ears - on a platter.

He alone carried the boar itself in on a very large platter, and finally he came in with the salt. Sir William carved the first few slices off both head and carcass before he handed the knife to the Stewart.

'Master Jacob's not here nor her Ladyship,'

Frog whispered as Sir William bent his head in silent prayer.

Prayer finished, the platters were handed round and then down the table. It was the ritual and the pecking order, I decided, which placed Sir William out of my reach. I did not think I would have the courage to approach him and ask after Jacob, I thought, when suddenly the servants went mad, shouting and banging empty tankards onto the wooden table.

Sir William rose.

He held up his hands.

'Thank you for your good wishes, my friends, and also for your kind attendance,' he said.

Good wishes? I wondered, when the two little girls started wailing. He smiled, tucked them into the crocks of his arms, and carried them upstairs.

As I listened to his treads resounding on the wooden steps - for the entire top part of the hall was built from wood onto the foundation of grey stone reaching up to a man's shoulders - I thought of poor Jacob running away from the noise his crutches made.

I did not blame him.

I would now have to be brave myself and approach Sir William, once more seated among his fine guests cracking walnuts as the servants were leaving the table. I wanted to find out how Jacob was.

Apart from which, I told Frog, I needed my coat for the night.

'I should think so,' he said. 'They're not short of a few coats.'

'Will you come with me?'

'If you want me to,' Frog said. 'They can only tell us to get lost. That's what it's all about.'

'What is?'

'Riches and power.'

He was right. The Saxmunds had the power to

make us jump, or not, as I would shortly find out. For the moment I was content. Anybody who fed their servants like Sir William did couldn't be all bad.

Chapter 17

I would be all right on my own, I told Frog, but I wished I had not lost my hat.

I could have twisted it, standing there waiting for somebody to notice me. My hands suddenly loomed large and as useless as lumps of lard.

As the ladies left the table and went upstairs, Sir William and the male guests moved over to the hearth. I was close behind them.

'Yes?' said the Stewart, nearly falling over me. His almost triangular, cat-like face bore a frown of impatience.

'I need to speak to Sir William,' I said wringing my hands. 'It's urgent. Most urgent. I'm Matthew. I met Jacob yesterday. I'm the new pot boy.'

'I think I have found the boy,' the Stewart said to Sir William, 'or rather he has found you. He's in your employ.'

'So,' Sir William said in his urgent, clipped tones as he turned to me. 'So. We have combed the countryside for you. I rode to Clare. I already had some business there, but I intended to ask Brother Aloysius if he knew anything of your whereabouts, but he had been and gone.'

Brother Aloysius was probably in one the villages, I gabbled on, looking after the sick. 'Mostly he can't affect a cure, but he does bring the sick a marvellous sense of comfort.'

Sir William favoured me with a look which said he didn't need a word to the wise from me.

'My Aunt Biddy says,' I added. 'How is Jacob?'

'Not well,' Sir William said. 'Not well at all. He has a fever. The physician is with him now.'

He turned to his guests and introduced me as the boy who had shown a true spirit of Christian brotherhood.

'Matthew lent my son his coat to keep him warm in the night.'

'Well,' I said, 'let's get this right, if you please. Jacob did say if he died I would get the blame. The scapegoat caught in the hedge.'

'Your Aunt Biddy says, no doubt.'

'Somebody else has to get the blame. Sounds like Jacob,' Sir William said.

He snapped his fingers, the Steward snapped his, and in no time at all I was clutching my coat.

'Come, Matthew,' Sir William said, leading me to the table and dismissing the maids trying to clear it. 'Sit down. Now tell me. What is all this nonsense about someone stealing Jacob's crutches? Methinks it was taken for firewood.'

'Firewood? In a forest full of what you might call firewood?'

I told him all about Eli, of the pleasure he would take in tormenting Jacob purely because he was my friend. How Brother Aloysius had been attacked by him when he had taken my place.

'So I can't go home until Eli is caught. I thought if we could get something with Eli's scent your hounds might find him. He is mighty good at ducking and weaving in the woods.'

Sir William looked at me thoughtfully.

'The woods are vast though and his scent could be lost by now. But if he reappears, as would seem likely, the hounds might hunt him down.'

I thought he would snap his fingers, command one of his servants to ride to Horringer to fetch something Eli had used and all would be speedily resolved.

'So, Matthew,' Sir William said. 'Be ready before first light. We'll ride to Horringer together.'

He rose.

'What now?' he added when I stood there with my mouth wide open.

'It's like this, if you don't mind. I can't ride,' I said. 'I might be able to forge a horseshoe out of a strip of iron eventually, but I wouldn't be able to ride the horse.'

He looked at me. Then he beckoned the Stewart.

'Robert,' he said. 'Can you be so good and ask Peter to get my horse ready and one of the milder ones - Percy, perhaps - before first light.'

Chapter 18

Sir William would see me in the morning before first light, I later told Frog glumly. Most likely he would see me falling off a horse, I added as we saw to the pots, platters, goblets and tankards.

The platters were the least trouble though. Frog and I carted them to the kennels and got the hounds to lick them clean.

'Hounds lick their pups after they're born, couldn't be cleaner,' he said, polishing each one on the sleeve of his jacket which was every bit as fine as mine, I told him.

We worked fast. The hounds barked and howled to get at the plates and before long somebody would come and investigate.

'I have some very good clothes,' Frog said, back in the kitchen, his eyes looking into the far distance. 'A maniac gave them to me.'

'A maniac?'

'Must have been. He suddenly turned up. He said he was my father and he wanted me to go with him. I told him I would rather not, I already had a father. Then he came back with these clothes.'

'You do have a father, I suppose.'

Frog shook his head.

'That was a lie to get rid of him. I was brought up by my step-brothers, I never knew my mother, or my father. I became a logger with one of my brothers. We got into a fight with the others and I came here.'

'And then?'

'Then nothing for a while, and then this maniac turned up, like I said. He asked if I ever had an illness leaving my skin like it is when I was about two.'

Frog didn't know.

'Then the maniac asked me what my proper

name was. I said I was Jonathan the tanner's grandson, and then he cried and said I was his son.'

He paused.

'But now I do believe he was my father.'

'What makes you think so?'

'He was tall and handsome and kind, so I'd like him to be.'

I laughed as I thought of my father, Frog's father and so my half-brother, but I was letting him in on it gently.

'Now they'll have two pot boys.'

There was only one, Frog said, which had been him and now it was me. He'd stay in the kitchen for a week to teach me the chores. And then he would become a stable-boy.

'There's not much to do as a rule, tonight's feast is an exception,' he said. 'A get-together for everybody, some feast day.'

Normally there was only the family and the indoor servants to feed, he added, and the servants ate in the kitchen.

It had to be a celebration for Jacob's safe return, I thought as I followed Frog out of the kitchen and into a huge divided barn.

'Our side is for men, t'other for maids.'

'The marrieds had cottages on the grounds,' he added, before he, like me, fell onto a sack not occupied by a snoring or cursing or farting form.

He fell asleep before I could explain properly that we shared a maniac father. Frog was probably the lost boy, my brother, I began, and then I too fell asleep.

I woke early as always, and made my way to the stables where I found Sir William already seated on a dark horse, its eyes shining magically in the glow cast by a torch that Peter, the head of stables as I found out later, held aloft.

'What a beautiful horse,' I said. 'Is it called Merlin?'

What made me say it I shall never know. Maybe it was to prolong the moment when I had to mount the horse Peter was holding.

'Moonshine, out of Merlin,' Peter said.

'It's sire was Merlin,' Sir William added.

'And yours is Percy,' Peter said.

'Percival for short?'

'The stable boy must have told Frog,' said the groom.

I was about to deny it, but Sir William grew impatient.

'Grab hold of the reins, Matthew. Left foot into the stirrup,' he said, 'Swing your right leg over the horse and move your body forward. Hold the reins, pull left for left, right for right, both together for straight on.'

'Are you nervous?' Sir William asked me.

'Terrified,' I admitted.

'Good,' he said. 'You must remember a horse is a live creature and has to be handled right. It must always be gently exercised before a long ride.'

You were also very high up on this live creature, I thought, my nervousness subsiding. Then an idea came to me.

I reversed the process.

I swung my right leg over to dismount.

It was as I had thought. The weight on dismounting was centred on my left leg, the same as in mounting

'What's he doing off?' Peter said when I mounted the horse gain, but we left him behind when Sir William slammed its rump. I did likewise and we rode off together.

I concentrated on a light canter, which again

112

wasn't difficult, so I told Sir William about my plan.

'Jacob wants to ride,' I said. 'And his good leg, his strong one, is his left one. He can swing the weak leg over easily enough. Somebody can help him mount and dismount. Frog might do it.'

Sir William promised to think about it.

'The right stirrup would need shortening, but his leg and thigh muscles are strong,' he said. 'But Jacob's mother might not go along with the idea. Not at the present time.'

Spending a night lost in the woods might be very few boys' idea of having the time of their lives, he added. It would be wonderful for Jacob to have an outdoor life and a friendship like he and Aloysius used to share.

He sighed.

'Now what's this about a frog in the kitchen and a frog in the stables? And do I really want to know?'

'Frog is the pot boy. He's going to be a stable-lad.'

'Frog. Odd name, but then all else about boys these days strikes me as exceedingly odd. No matter. Do you feel up to a trot?'

He didn't wait for an answer, but urged me to watch him.

As the horse rose, I brought my knees up and together, letting them fall loosely, and up again, following its rhythm.

'Gallop?' I shouted.

'I think not. Perhaps on the way back when you can gauge the terrain. Look out for uneven ground, mole holes, and any kind of obstruction.'

Riding was wonderful, seeing the world from this height, the horse's neck in front rising and falling with me, its ears pricked up with the sheer joy of it.

'Well done Matthew,' Sir William said. 'I

believe we are in Horringer. I'm in your hands now.'

Feeling an excitement rising in me along with the coming light of dawn, we dismounted by the forge, fastening the horses to the tying post.

'Please excuse me, Sir William. I won't be a minute,' I said. 'I have an almighty surprise in store for somebody.'

Chapter 19

Mattie was in the yard, lowering a bucket down the well. Waiting for it to fill up, she yawned, stuffing her knuckles into her mouth to stifle it.

'Let me pull it up for you,' I cried, springing forward.

'God, you gave me such a fright. What are you doing here?'

I said it was a long story.

'How's it going here and at home? What's your new boy like? Has my grandmother died yet?' I added.

'Nothing's altered and your grandmother is as ever. Are you mad? I'm not sure I want you to whistle for me.'

'Why not?'

'YOU'VE ONLY BEEN GONE FOR TWO DAYS!'

Two days! It seemed more like two years.

'I have ridden over with Sir William Saxmund of Exning,' I said as modestly as I could, studying my fingernails.

'As you do if you can't ride and don't know him,' she said, grabbing my hands. 'Honestly! Now's not the time to go mad, it's not safe here. They haven't found Eli yet.'

I told her that was precisely the long story I hadn't got the time for. I took her to the front of the house where we found Sir William pacing up and down, patting Moonshine and Percy, slapping his hands together in a flurry of impatience.

'I'm Matilda,' she said, pushing her wonderful red hair behind her ears. 'Mother will be mad that I haven't got my cap on. You must be the Sir William I thought Matthew was kidding me about.'

She listened, hands behind her back as he

explained we needed something with Eli's scent for the hounds.

She shook her head.

'There's nowt.'

'How about his bed?'

'Mother burned it,' she said. 'It was but a sack filled with straw.'

'No matter, but think on,' he said, untying the horses. 'Let us away to meet your parents, Matthew. If Eli is watching your home all the better. He will see you are under my protection.'

'You might draw attention to yourself,' Matilda cried. 'The horses will be safe enough here. I'll rouse my father. Wait here.'

Sir William shook his head as if his brain was addled.

'As I've said, the youth of today is a new breed,' he said as we finally walked through the village waking to a new day. 'That girl seems to have a bit of Saxon with her sapphire eyes and red-gold hair.'

'Sapphire eyes?'

'Gem stones. Very rare.'

Matilda might have a bit of Saxon in her, but what of me with my dark hair and light-brown eyes?

'Who knows,' Sir William said. 'It wasn't only Saxons who invaded England. There were the Jutes and the Angles, and the Romans.'

'And I might take after the natives, whoever they were,' I said, when I noticed the Saxon maid with the gemstone eyes racing past us.

'I better warn your family. Tell 'em you're coming, I mean,' she cried over her shoulder.

Everybody was up and about. The door to our cottage opened and Boy shot out, straight into my arms, whimpering with pleasure. I looked up, and there was my mother, as pretty as any of the ladies I had seen dining the night before.

Prettier.

I walked towards her.

'I should put that dog down first if I were you,' said Biddy after the introductions, and everything was as it had always been. Even my father wasn't there. He was apparently in Bury, trying to rouse the sheriff to take action against Eli.

The beds had been shaken out, fresh rushes had been laid, grandmother was up and dressed, the porridge was bubbling on the stove and the sun had risen over the horizon as we sat at the table, breakfasting.

'We had a disturbed night with my mother, Sir William, she got us very early,' Biddy explained after the explanations of how I came to be in such high company.

My grandmother's disturbed night was fortunate, it seemed to me, the cottage was neat. Nobody walked around in an early-morning daze yawning and scratching themselves, and Sir William looked about him as if he was in heaven.

'This is perfect, just perfect. This is what I often dream about. I've always had a longing for the simple life,' he said.

'What a coincidence, so have I,' said Biddy, curling her lip.

'I dare say it's not as simple as that.'

My mother smiled.

'We have a roof over our heads, our health and strength and each other,' she said. 'And the continuation.'

Sir William looked briefly at my grandmother who was happily talking to herself.

'Just so,' he said, 'the continuation. I had to put

117

my house in order for future generations. Also my station in life imposes certain obligations on me with my servants and tenants.'

He sighed.

'I'm to join King Edward's army abroad next week.'

I was in shock. What on earth would they do on that estate without him giving the orders??

I finally came to when he turned the talk towards Brother Aloysius and Clare.

'I rode over to Clare and told my brother of my imminent departure,' he said.

'And how is the Blessed Abbot?' I cried. 'Did you take him any grapes?'

'Manners, Matthew,' my mother cried.

'Don't you remember, mother? We had grapes in Clare, and we got thrown off the cart by a monk. "I'll give you eating the Blessed Abbot's grapes," he said. He was one mean monk.'

'None meaner than a monk in bad mood,' Sir William said.

'Or a nun,' said my mother, 'although I don't think every monk and every nun had a calling and wants to be there.'

As the talk turned towards nuns and monks and their calling or not, I slipped out of the cottage to talk to Mattie. I told her when Eli had been caught I would come back and stay, for ever and ever.'

We talked about life as a pot boy, about my new friend, Frog, Sir William, and about Jacob.

'I thought the celebrations were a thanksgiving for Jacob's safe return, but it was to give Sir William a chance to say a proper goodbye,' I concluded.

Mattie said it would be a wonderful sight to see him ride off in his shining armour, I was to tell her all about it, but as it turned out there was nothing to tell. I never saw him go. In fact, nobody saw Sir William leave early one morning.

As for the armour, that was already abroad, waiting for him with his retinue - his most trusted friends and servants - which included the Stewart, Frog said a few days later.

Retinue. It had a good ring to it so I memorised it.

'I'll look after your dog when I go the stables,' Frog added. 'Cook doesn't look kindly on him hanging around your feet in the kitchen.'

Boy had followed me from a distance, ignoring my commands to turn back, until Sir William had picked him up and put him in his saddle bag. Now he laid by me feet, the two yellow fangs protruding from his black muzzle giving him an odd look, as if he knew a joke we hadn't been let in on.

'Pot boy,' the cry went up, just as I was demonstrating my amazing way with fires to the cook.

'Soft wood for a blaze, hard wood for simmering.'

'Pot boy. That'll be Frog,' she said. 'You're wanted upstairs.'

'At last,' Frog said, ramming his hat over his head. 'When I come back I'll be a stable lad.'

Or not. He was back in no time.

'What happened?'

'They want you,' he said glumly. 'Jacob threw a fit when he saw me. You're not a pot boy,' he screamed. 'Go away. I want Matthew.'

Jacob must be feeling better, I thought.

'Alec is there,' Frog said. 'He is Jacob's tutor.'

'That's right,' Martha said. 'He's a scribe now as well.'

'What does a scribe do?'

'He scribes, I suppose.'

'He keeps the accounts and sees to the wages and taxes now Robert is no longer stewarting,' Cook said. 'I expect Jacob'll turn blue in the face if you don't turn up soon.'

I took the hint and asked Frog to show me the way.

The dog was close at my heels as we crossed a few passages, went through the chamber and up the stairs. I knocked on the door Frog pointed out, when Jacob's two small sisters appeared from nowhere and attached themselves silently to us.

'Come,' a deep voice said. It was Alec, the scribe or tutor, I saw when I opened the door and we all went in.

The chamber was large.

The light forcing its way through the glass panes shone on the lady sitting on a chair. A lady dressed in grey stood behind her. The seated lady's hands were folded in her lap, her lips were clamped tight shut.

So this was the Lady Isabel who had captured Brother Aloysius's heart.

She wore a green gown, not unlike my mother's that had been dyed with nettles, but hers was shinier. Her head was covered in some sort of a cloth of the same colour. She had a long face, a low forehead and dark brown eyes. She was very pale. She resembled a sheep, and if she was a great disappointment to me - who thought all ladies and princesses and queens had no right to be plain - I don't suppose she cared.

'What is all this?' she said, pointing to the dog and Frog hovering by my side. 'And where is your nurse, my naughty young ladies?'

The girls looked at each other as if they were strangers to the word 'nurse'.

'This my retinue,' my lady,' I ventured after some thought. 'The girls you know about. But the dog is Boy, and the boy is Frog.'

'Methinks I am losing my senses,' Lady Isabel said to the scribe. 'Can you make....'

She was interrupted by Jacob. He was sitting on a window seat.

'Ask him why he isn't wearing a hat, mother,' he cried.

'Why are you not wearing a hat?' the lady forced through her clenched teeth.

'He's not wearing a hat because he lost it in the woods,' Jacob cried. 'It's a riddle, maybe it's not a very good one.'

He got up and came towards me.

'Look, Matthew, no crutches, just a walking stick. Isn't it a good thing I met you that night?'

He stopped and looked at Frog.

'I want to ask you something,' he said to him. 'Don't you mind looking like you do?'

'Well no, I don't,' Frog said. 'I don't know what I look like, you see. I've never looked at myself.'

'So you don't know you're ugly,' Jacob said. 'You don't have to look at yourself but I do, so it's my hard luck.'

'But it's not mine,' I cried. 'Frog is my most excellent friend.'

Lady Isabel's mouth flew open. 'Nobody in this world is ever ugly. A fine world it would be if we were all alike. As for you, Jacob, I am most displeased. *Noblesse Oblige*. Every time you reach out...'

'Reach out? How would I know about reaching out? I'm not allowed to go out. You say nobody is ugly, but you're ashamed of me. Even Matthew, a pot boy, has a retinue of sorts.'

Lady Isabel threw her soft hands up in the air.

'I aim to stop you from getting hurt,' she said.

She lowered her hands and pointed a finger at us. Then she began to laugh, and when she did, the severe mask of her face cracked.

'Matthew and his retinue. Have you ever seen anything so comical in all your life, Alec?' she asked the tutor.

He probably had, for his face never cracked.

Boy sighed.

He laid down with his head between his paws and ground his teeth. When he rolled his eyes I knew it would be followed by a blood-curdling howl;. it was time to leave.

Jacob accompanied us, asking his mother very prettily for leave to do so, but Frog and I were not impressed.

'I'm sorry I was rude,' Jacob cried. 'But I was so disappointed. I wanted to have you to myself, Matthew. Never mind. Let me show you how well I use my stick.'

And he did use it well. He put his weight onto his left leg. Moving the stick onto the next rung not straight ahead but to the side, if he fell he would not tumble head over heels but land on the next rung and against the rail.

It took some time, but finally we were standing in the ante-chamber. Boy was getting impatient. I thought he had a mind to lift his leg against Jacob's stick so I let him out.

'Matthew,' Jacob said, when I returned. 'I want you to promise me something. Listen carefully.This is important.'

'Anything, Jacob,' I said, dreading what was coming. Did he want me to share his chamber? His lessons? Run after him and fulfil his every whim?

'As you know, my father is away. I want you to promise me your allegiance until my father returns.'

I had already promised Mattie I would return when it was safe.

'Only until Sir William returns?'

'I'll set you free and let you go home when he comes back, or until I release you from your promise.'

I sighed with relief.

Sir William would return, the war in France had to end soon. Eli would be caught and I would return to Horringer.

'I'll be your master,' Jacob said.

'And I'll be your man.'

'Until his father gets back,' Frog said, who had enough. 'I don't suppose you'll want a priest for a witness?'

Jacob considered it.

His pretty, fine-featured face, surrounded by a halo of golden curls, wore a deep frown.

'No,' he said. 'You'll do. In fact, it's better. Jacob and Matthew and...I can't call you Frog, though, if you are part of my retinue.'

But Frog it was, or nothing.

'So be it. Jacob and Matthew and Frog. The thing is,' he added, 'Gavin de Vere is coming over and I need somebody on my side. Gavin thinks he is better than me. In fact, he thinks a cripple in the family is a disgrace.'

'You're not a cripple, you'e a Saxmund, Jacob. I mean, a de Vere better than a Saxmund?' Frog cried. 'You have to be joking. The three of us will soon show him. Don't you worry.'

Chapter 20

'Who are the de Veres?' Frog asked when we made our way back to the kitchen.

I had heard of them..

'I believe they endow the monastery in Clare.'

'Frog laughed.

'I suppose the brothers have to live somewhere. I had no idea, I just wanted to get out of Jacob's way. Rude boy.'

'Spoilt and not happy,' I agreed, 'he thinks everybody looks at him and checks if one leg is still shorter than the other, except they no loner notice it.'

Jacob was brave. He had tackled those huge stairs as if they were nothing, but that wasn't all. He had also told Frog he was ugly.

Frog might be short, but he was also powerfully strong, but he wouldn't hit a boy in front of his mother, he said.

'Your name didn't help,' I told him. 'But now Jacob is used to it. He just doesn't think before he speaks, a bit like me,' I added. 'Me and my big mouth and my liking for big words like "retinue." I don't know what sort of a mess it'll end me up in next. Wherever it is, it'll do me no good.'

Frog disagreed.

'If you have words, don't keep them to yourself.'

He slapped me on my back.

'You have to use everything you have to survive. You made her Ladyship laugh, and now we are in.'

We were in.

In the stables, that is, where we mucked out, fed the horses, learnt to saddle and put reins and halters on them and took them out for an early trot.

We polished their saddles, and sometimes we were allowed to exercise them in the afternoon with the grooms.

We looked after the hounds kept in four kennels, and we slept in the tack room, Frog and I. We worked and ate and slept side by side, and we discussed everything under the sun, Boy always by our side.

We talked so much that everybody called us 'the two old maids', but we didn't care. We decided life was about keeping warm and fed, companionship and family. I was certain Frog was my half-brother, the lost boy my father had searched for, for so long.

'He travelled all over the place to find you,' I cried. 'How old are you, Frog?'

He was between fifteen or sixteen, he said, but it wasn't easy finding anybody who didn't want to be found. Villagers played dumb to inquisitive strangers, and to my huge surprise, *not everybody liked the Austin Friars*.

If I was overjoyed to have an older brother, Frog was pleased to have a friend of his own age, more or less.

He had more than enough brothers of his own, he said. They were all a grumpy lot, much older and handy with a belt to tan his backside. Some were married with children.

'Sixteen living at home,' Frog said. 'You couldn't move without falling over somebody. I can't stand being cooped up now and nobody else liked us. But you see, my father was a tanner.'

'Have you ever seen or smelt a tanner?' he added.

Apparently a tanner was yellow and he smelt like the putrid meat he scraped off the hides. Tanners were outcasts.

Maybe Jacob was like a younger brother and friend to us, or maybe not, but we certainly had our work cut out to look after him at times.

Sometimes Jacob was allowed to ride with us, as I had suggested to Sir William, and he soon became a good rider, but he was also headstrong. He wasn't allowed to ride on his own ON PAIN OF DEATH, or join the hunt, or gallop, Alec - his tutor - impressed on Frog and me more than once.

But what did Alec know of life in the stables?

He was a pale man of letters, more boy than man though. He was a short man, he had a high forehead over which his blond hair fell in loose strands.

Pain of death. It was only an expression, we told ourselves. But whose death exactly? I didn't give much thought to Eli until one night, about a month later. Boy had got used to the night noises, the hounds occasional yelps, the sudden stamping of a restless horse, the chirping of a nightjar.

So when we were roused by Boy's sharp barking, we stumbled outside into the dark.

The hounds went mad in the kennels and before long the yard was filled with all manner of folk adding to the din.

Boy looked up at the stable roof, barking hysterically at a white barn owl.

'Steady on. It's only an owl, Boy,' I said, but I recalled the night Eli had perched on the blacksmith's roof.

And then my heart sank; I found a piece of bloody venison.

The hounds were harmless enough as a rule, but the scent of blood would have turned them into killers if I had been thrown into their kennel after the raw meat was flung in.

At breakfast the next morning, cook said one of

her meat pies and cheeses had gone walk-about.

'We'll have to lock the doors in future,' she said, and what was the world coming to, looking at the new pot boy suspiciously. She never trusted him from thereon and made his life pure and sheer hell, and that was Eli's work. He spoiled people's lives even from a distance, I said to Frog.

We kept our eyes and ears open from then on, although there were no more signs of Eli.

Sometimes Frog and I rose early. St John's Wort was in full bloom, carrying its yellow flowers like golden crowns set onto cushions of green. It made me think of Biddy. I just had to go and see Brother Aloysius and ask about my family.

We worked hard, but when the sun was at its height, Frog and I laid in the meadows behind the paddocks, hearing the grass grow, or so it seemed as we listened to the insects buzzing lazily amongst the greenery.

'Hot, isn't it,' said Jacob, sitting down next to us.

'The thing is, I am in trouble.'

'What sort of trouble?'

'We are entertaining the de Veres next week. On Saturday.'

'So?' I said as casually as I could. I remembered the last time guests had been entertained.

'I have to do the honours in my father's stead. Lead the party downstairs, that sort of thing. Just look at my hands.'

He held his hands out, trembling like dry leaves in an autumn gale. 'But have something in hand apart from the trembling,' he added.

'Underhand, you mean,' I said. 'Like going missing?'

Jacob nodded glumly.

'Steady on, Jacob,' Frog said. 'I mean you are a Saxmund. Just who do these de Veres think they are?'

'My mother is a de Vere. Their motto is *"Noblesse Oblige"*. Gavin de Vere is my noble cousin. He thinks I don't amount to much.'

'And does he?' I asked.

'He is tall and handsome. He rides to hounds. He has Latin, Greek, German and French.'

'But no English,' cried Frog.

'And English, of course.'

We gave the matter some thought.

If you knew you would come across a pack of wild dogs it was best to arm yourself with a stout stick and a few stones, Frog and I decided.

Maybe Jacob could wait for his guests and the ladies in the ante-chamber.

'You could avoid the stairs and when you thank everybody and repeat what your father said. What did he say when you last attended?'

'Bring in the boar's head. Wassail my friends. Tell the musicians to strike up. Well, it was Christmas.'

It wasn't Christmas now.

'What exactly did my father say at the last feast when I had the fever?'

'Thank you for your good wishes, my friends, and also for your kind attendance.'

Alec came up behind us and told Jacob his mother wanted him.

'Methinks you have more to do than lay in the grass all day,' he told Frog and I, but really he had no idea what went on in the stables.

'We've seen to the horses and dogs,' I said, getting up to show proper respect. 'All bar the raddling and skidaddling.'

'Get on with it then,' he said impatiently.

Jacob laughed and looked less tormented, but it

didn't last.

By the time Saturday arrived, we had moved from being anxious to terrified to suffering the torments of hell for him.

In the evening, Frog and I filed with the rest of the servants into the eating hall with scarcely a thought of the food covering the table.

'Jacob isn't in the ante-chamber,' Frog whispered as we stood by our places waiting for Jacob and his guests to join us, when we heard voices from afar. It seemed to take an age, but finally Jacob and his guests came down the stairs from the gallery leading into the ante-chamber and then into the hall.

We sat down when they were seated. Alec, in the Stewart's place, brought in a large platter of roasted venison, and finally he came in with the salt.

Jacob rose.

Leaning against the table, he carved the first few slices before he handed the knife to Alec.

So far, so good, I thought as the meal progressed, when the servants started to shout and bang their empty tankards onto the wooden table.

Jacob held up the one hand he didn't support himself with.

'Thank you for your good wishes my friends, and also for your kind attendance.'

His mother looked radiant with pride whereas one of Jacob's little sisters nodded off and fell face-forward into her custard.

A sneer disfigured Gavin de Vere's bony face, which might have been handsome on a horse.

Jacob rose.

'Please stay seated, my friends,' he said.

I could see now that he was angry he was no longer acting a part.

'I'll see my sisters off to their beds. If you

please, nurse.'

As we listened to the nurse and the little girls treads on the stairs and the click of Jacob's walking stick, Frog and I exhaled.

Suddenly hungry, we fell on the food when Alec approached us.

I looked up and saw Jacob was once more seated among his fine guests, cracking walnuts with Gavin de Vere.

'Now then, Matthew. I believe you want to see Brother Aloysius. Master Jacob wants me to tell you that you may ride over to Clare tomorrow morning. With Frog. You two may ride Percival and Joyous, I'll have a word with Peter at the stables,' Alec said.

He winked at me.

'Mind you see to your raddling and skidaddling first.'

We had been rumbled by Alec but he trusted us.

Sir William would return soon, pray God, and I would be able to go home. In the meantime, I would enjoy my time here with Frog, my brother. I knew he wouldn't come with me to the smithy. He couldn't abide being cooped up.

So I relaxed completely, although a child of three knows if it relaxes it will fall face-down into the custard. Or worse, into the fire, the dragon's breath.

Chapter 21

'Yes?' Brother Anselm at the priory in Clare said next morning, sticking his long nose through the peep-hole.

'Brother Aloysius?' I enquired.

'No. I'm not.'

'Is he here?'

'He might be, and then he might not. Especially if you are horse thieves. And keep that dog away from me.'

Boy, who had come along for the ride in my saddle bag, showed him his teeth.

'We're stable lads of Sir William's. We know these horses,' Frog said. 'One horse is called Percival, and the other Joyous.'

'Joyous is named after you,' I said.

'I wouldn't be joyous,' Brother Anselm said, 'if I suffered with my bones like he did.'

He opened the door.

'You seem familiar, but don't tell me. I never forget a face.'

'I'm Matthew, the cooper's son.'

'Never heard of you,' he said.

Then he shut the door into our faces.

I went to Confession and Mass in the town church while Frog stayed with Boy and looked after the horses.

When I came out of the church, Frog was chatting to Brother Aloysius.

He would ride with us for a while, Brother Aloysius said beaming at me, before he headed off to Horringer.

'I can tell your father you two brothers are good friends,' he said. 'But Frog. What an awful name to carry about for a fine fellow. And to think of the amount of times I have passed your family by.'

He wasn't to know, Frog said. 'My family detest the brothers,' he added. 'They think they are idle lay-abouts and scroungers who ought to be stoned.'

'That's why I used to pass by in a hurry thinking most un-Christian thoughts,' Brother Aloysius said.

'Oh yes? Like what?' I enquired.

'Like wishing a plague of pimples onto their sagging backsides,' he said, 'but nothing life-threatening. Never mind that now. How did Jacob's birthday celebrations go?'

'Birthday celebrations? Is that what it was? But I really want to know about the war before you leave us, Brother Aloysius. Will it end soon?'

'The war,' he sighed. 'Hopefully it would end soon. Edward is preparing for the final battle in France, a messenger said, and then conclude a treaty.'

A treaty.

It looked like we had to conclude one with Jacob who came galloping towards us after we had bid the brother farewell.

Jacob was in a foul mood.

My heart sank.

What happened to his triumph of the night before?

'The thing is,' he said, slowing down and trotting beside us, 'I wish my father was here. Gavin insulted me. He asked me the riddle of the Sphinx. I didn't understand it in Greek, and when I understood it in English, I didn't want to.'

The Sphinx was some kind of a mute, mythical beast, he explained.

I didn't pay much attention. I remembered Eli and his riddles.

'Now you look like a boy what likes riddles.

Am I right, boy? Well, here's one specially for you. What has you and the fire got in common? You have to breath to stay alive. You need air for living. Like the fire needs air for burning, you might say. About two minutes without air should do it. The boy died in his sleep, folks will say.

'You better listen to the riddle, Matthew,' Jacob said. 'I'm not repeating it.'

'What animal has four legs in the morning, two at noon, and three in the evening?'

'Do you give up?' he asked us after a while.
We nodded.
The animal, Gavin had told Jacob, was Man.
It was Man's life cycle.
First comes his youth; as a baby he crawls = four legs.
Then in his prime; at noon he walks upright = two legs.
Then old age; in the evening he walks with the help of a stick = three legs.
'And then I hit Gavin because I use a stick and I'm not an old man and he fell down. I hit him a bit more while I was at it to even old scores, and now I'm in disgrace for abusing our guest.'

'He deserved it, but they'll get over it,' Frog predicted confidently, but Jacob wasn't too sure when we parted from him at the stables.

Boy wasn't anywhere to be seen. Maybe he was resting in the shadow of a tree, I said as we mucked out when a shadow fell across the stable.

'I cannot find a groom. You there, boy. Saddle my horse. And look sharp about it.'

Frog and I put our pitch forks down and went

outside.

'If it isn't the noble Gavin,' I said.

Peter, head of stables, was within earshot, and I wanted him to hear what was going on.

'Gavin's got a good face for a horse, but we shouldn't insult horses, I suppose,' I said, chancing my luck.

'I believe you're right,' Frog said. 'Just as well Jacob re-arranged his face.'

'Jacob punched me,' Gavin cried. 'It wasn't fair. I wasn't expecting it.'

'Jacob wasn't expecting to be insulted and called an old man just because he uses a walking stick,' I cried. 'Go on, tell Peter the riddle of the Sphinx you asked Jacob.'

'It might be a good idea,' Peter said, coming forward. We were good lads as a general rule, he added. We would also know the consequences would be worse than awful if we had been rude to Gavin.

'Speak, master Gavin,' Peter thundered.

'What animal has four legs in the morning, two at noon and three in the evening?' Gavin mumbled.

'Explain,' thundered Peter.

'Man's life cycle. The baby crawls, four legs. He walks upright, two legs. He walks with a stick, three legs.'

'So you called him an old man.'

'I meant to impress Jacob with my understanding of Greek. I was showing off, I suppose. It dawned on me what I was saying when I came to the last line and by then it was too late.'

He was riding home to fetch his bow and arrow for Jacob, he added nervously, as Jacob was so marvellously strong in the shoulders.

'Go to it then, make amends,' Peter said. 'Saddle his horse, Matthew. Get on with your chores, Frog.'

Left alone with Gavin, I looked up at him, seated on his horse.

'That was quick thinking, master Gavin,' I said.

'Yes, wasn't it,' he said proudly. 'But Jacob is welcome to my best bow.'

'Because he won't be able to stand and shoot an arrow?'

There was that to it, he said.

'You've got a big mouth, boy, way above your station,' he said before he rode off. 'It'll end you up in trouble one of these days.'

He was right. I had a big mouth, always had. It would end me up in trouble. Just how much trouble I would find out very shortly.

Chapter 22

Frog was walking Martha home that evening. A herd of wild pigs had been seen in the open. Martha's mother was very ill. She had received the Last Rites and they intended to come back in the morning.

Frog didn't want to ask for permission in case we had overdone the favours, so I did his share of the work and missed the dinner bell.

Boy was still missing.

I wandered into the kitchen when my stomach started to rumble.

'And what sort of time do you call this?' cook whined at me as she came out of the provisions room.

'Time? Who knows the time?'

'I do. It's past your dinner time, my lad,' she said. 'Just been counting the loaves and pies.'

She had a strange experience in the woods, she said. She'd been collecting fungi. Her basket was full when she put it to the ground and reached up to cut a Chicken-of-the-woods growing out of a tree trunk.

A Chicken-of-the-woods fungus was reddish-brown, looked like a puffed-up chicken and was tasty on meatless Fridays.

'When I turned round, my basket was still there but it was empty,' she said. 'Somebody played a trick on me.'

'It weren't me,' said the pot boy, Mark. 'It weren't me either when that meat pie went missing.'

It might not have been, but he got an almighty wallop from cook.

I would have a word with Martha when she came back I thought as the boy slowly got up,, but I had other, more urgent things on my mind.

Was it Eli playing tricks, I wondered, leaving the kitchen. It was late. A full harvest moon hung in the sky like a ripe fruit when I took one last turn around the meadow behind the stables, the last to be mown.

One minute I looked restlessly at the moon and inhaled the meadow's spicy scent, the next I felt a sharp knock and then a pain on the back of my head. Stars danced in front of my eyes and then I fell into a black hole of oblivion.

When I came to, I thought I was paralysed. I was doubled up and I could not move neither my arms of my legs nor could I talk, but I could hear Boy whimpering feebly from a distance.

When I forced my eyes open I saw my arms and hands were tied around my knees. A cloth was fastened tightly across my mouth.

I saw all this through a fire flickering brightly in a hole in the ground, illuminating the darkness around it.

Eli was squatting by the fire, stirring a pot on it.

'He's awake at last. I thought I might have hit him too hard. It's hard to know exactly how much force to use on a young skull so as not to break it.'

He chuckled.

'And I don't want to break it just yet. I haven't had the entertainment yet. Well, here he is, that good boy, your so-called friend, young master,' he said.

I turned my head and saw Jacob next to me, trussed up like I was, staring at me sideways.

'Only he ain't your friend, young master. You wouldn't be here otherwise, but that's how it is with this here boy.'

He ladled out some of the stew into a bowl.

'Look at me, young master, when I'm talking to you.'

Eli smiled when Jacob kept on looking at me.

'Spirit. I like that. It gives spice to the torment. The trouble is, you might say, this here good boy

Matthew is always ready to do his duty. And for why? He likes to be a good boy so he can get his feet under a table. Any table will do for him. Do you see any kind of a table here, boy?'

He blew on the stew.

'Answer me, or I'll throw this hot potage into your face.'

I made some strangled noises behind the cloth.

He laughed.

'It's a good job I'm an even-tempered kind of a man, or else I might take offence at these noises you call talking. I best do the talking myself. Where do you think you are?'

In a hut in a forest, I wanted to say. Or some kind of a hut.

Hazel twigs were bound together and formed a low roof over a hole.

'Wherever it is, you can't see it from above. I made the deep pit, see? The young master couldn't get up the side on his backside, if young masters have backsides, when I went to get you.'

The hounds will get our scent, I thought.

Eli shook his head, reading my thoughts.

'Forget the hounds. This forest has a lot of little streams running right through it.'

Eli slurped his potage.

'Mushrooms and wood pigeons. Very tasty. You should have seen that fat woman's face when her mushrooms had vanished.'

He grinned and shook his head.

Then he put his bowl down.

'They'll find you eventually, two pretty boys laying dead side by side,' he said. 'I've had all summer to prepare it. When you got nice and cosy at the hall, you might say, always such a pretty, clean boy and always ready with the smart answer, I got ready for the entertainment.'

He stood up and came towards us.

'It's that dog who was the dratted nuisance, yap, yap, yap. I was going to throw you to the hounds with the venison, but I got him today and his throat will be cut if you don't behave..'

Eli stared into our faces.

'That there boy with the smart answer, the big mouth, is mighty silent, ain't he? Smart. He knows better than to be rude, don't he. Calls himself a boy, he does, but he's more sensible than an old woman. And for why?'

He took his hat off and scratched himself.

'I'll tell you for why. He has to be well-in wherever he goes. Riding horses with his nose up in the air now,' he said to Jacob, grabbing him under his chin. 'But here's a riddle. If he's so important, how come nobody's missed him? Who exactly pines for him?'

Who?

'Who?' the owl asked politely from outside. 'Who? Who?'

Eli released Jacob and went outside.

When he came back, he threw some more wood onto the fire.

'They'll miss you tomorrow, and they'll miss the young master, but that's as far as it goes. Life goes on. It goes on for the boy's family. His mother is smiling as sweetly as ever. The blacksmith has another boy, Matilda drives the boys mad with her pretty ways. As for that interfering monk, he rides through the villages without a thought for him.'

Eli chuckled.

'You might say life goes on in the same old way, that same old way he messed up for me.'

He picked up a knife.

He came towards us and pulled one of my hairs

out.

'Hold this between your fingers,' he said.

'I suppose you can't,' he added. 'But take it from me a knife has to be sharp to slice through it.'

He moved to the other side of the fire with the knife.

'Bear it in mind. I'm having a little nap now. The entertainment is going too fast for my liking. I would have liked to steal a horse and food from the hall, but I had to lie low after that yappy dog gave me away. And for why?'

He looked at me.

'I aimed for surprise.'

He yawned.

'I'm bone tired, which is the boy's fault. I had to carry the dog here. And then the young master. And then that good boy with all the answers which some might call a big mouth.'

He laid down and shut his eyes.

Jacob and I looked at each other, but we dared not move.

If my big mouth was one weapon, my other one was touching the ribbon to summon Morgan Le Fey.

I had to get my hands free, but how? I wondered, when nature gave me a helping hand.

'I have to go,' I whined through the gag.

Jacob whined as well.

'Dratted boys,' Eli said, opening a space of the roof and pushing me out of it. 'I don't mind my own stink but I can't abide yours.'

He freed my hands, told me the dog would get if I tried anything, threw me into some bushes and told me to get on with it, which I did. Then I took the gag out of my mouth.

I breathed deeply and felt in my breeches for the ribbon, when I felt a sharp kick in my back.

'I'll give you knife, you vermin,' Eli said, a great black figure towering over me.

Then he laughed

'A ribbon. Did I say you were like an old woman? More like a maid, if you ask me.'

He put the ribbon in his pocket, tied my hands behind my back and threw me back into the pit.

'You'll have your hands free so take your gag out,' I whispered as Eli lowered himself into our prison.

'And now for the young master,' he said.

Poor Jacob! What had I got him into? I thought when I heard a scuffle and scream. Two screams!

Next Jacob was thrown in. His hands were tied now, but he had taken his gag out. His face was covered in blood. He didn't move and he looked dead.

'Not dead, more's the pity,' Eli said coming down. 'Just look at my hand. That's what he did.'

A bright gash across one of his hands spurted blood.

'Good job it's the left one,' he muttered, wrapping it with a cloth, and then he knocked Jacob's old crutches into the ground with the reverse side of an axe.

'I knew they would come in handy,' he said, tying our hands over our heads to the crutches.

Silence and darkness fell, broken only by the odd snort from Eli and the odd dying spark off the fire.

'Please God, please Jacob, please, please don't die,' I whispered.

'I wouldn't give him the satisfaction,' the tiniest whisper floated across to me. 'I had a knife on my belt. I might have to go, but I am going to take him with me as sure as my name is Jacob Saxham of Exning.'

'Who? Who?' the owl asked.

Eli jumped up, cursed the owl and us and sat there, an evil presence.

Jacob was right. If we had to die, we would die well. We would try and take Eli with us.

I fell asleep without the slightest idea how we could get the better of him.

Chapter 23

Once the fire went out, the night settled over us like a black crow spreading its wings over a nest, but finally a rosy dawn forced some of its faint light into our prison.

Jacob looked pale and I felt him shivering next me when Eli rose, and with some difficulty.

He made the fire up first.

When it took hold with a cluster of red sparks, he crawled outside.

I stared at the fire. If ever Morgan le Fey was needed it was now, but however hard I looked there was no blue at the heart of the yellow flames.

When Eli slithered in, he gave us a filthy look and he came over with the gag.

'You don't want to shove this into my mouth,' I said.

'Oh? Is that so. Why not, vermin?'

'I'll tell you after you've given us some water.'

'And why should I do that?'

'Because you must have been very bored all summer with nobody to torment. Now you would like to hear my voice begging you to leave off.'

Never had water been more welcome even if most of it was running down our chins as it was forced into our faces.

'Eli seems to think we're very helpless without arms, don't you think, Matthew?' Jacob said.

His right eye was closed and the skin around bruised.

It seemed to please Eli by the smirk on his face.

'Helpless but not hopeless,' I said. 'Life might go on without me, but everybody is always glad to see the back of Eli. You see, nobody has any respect for him.'

'And why is that, boy?'

'Because you are mean and you stink worse than an old tom cat.'

Jacob and I looked at each other.

'Eli's ignorant as well,' I said. 'He doesn't know your father is under the king's protection.'

Eli sat down. He wasn't moving too well. Maybe his bones ached.

'The young master might be. The boy's wrong.'

'That's what you think,' Jacob cried. 'Matthew is in my father's employ and under his care and this country isn't big enough for you to hide in.'

Eli sighed.

'That boy with all the answers hasn't done you much good, young master. Your father is abroad. Nobody will find your graves, not even the king himself, and I'll be long gone.'

He sighed.

'I'm weary, living outside's done it. The sport isn't as good as I thought it was. It's being penned up down here all this time that's done my bones in.'

He threw another log onto the fire. It was sparking as red as Mattie's hair in the half-gloom of the hut, and then I saw it, the blue at the heart of the flame.

I stiffened. *Eli had said something of importance*, but what was it?

'Didn't you hear me, boy?' he said, raising his voice. 'You've not done me much good. Being penned up here all this time has done it to my bones.'

I exhaled slowly.

TIME!

Time had hurt Eli's bones, *all this time*.

Time was destructive. Time ate through things just like a fire and destroyed them, I thought, when Eli approached me.

'It's time to rearrange you, boy,' he said, 'or disarrange might be a better way of putting it.'

I now had trouble breathing for I suddenly felt deathly afraid.

Not only for myself but for everybody. To play around with time was too dangerous.

I had to divert him. I somehow had to make him cut the ropes binding me, and then I had to attack him. But how?

Chapter 24

'Oh, please, Eli,' I cried. 'Don't take my jacket. Not that. You can do anything you like but please, please, don't burn my jacket. It's the only thing I've got I can call my own.'

'Your jacket? Is that so?'

He chuckled.

'I wasn't born yesterday. I would have to cut you loose, and I haven't reckoned on doing that. Or maybe I will. I'll burn all your clothes for the sport. Think how cold you'll be in your graves.'

He cut our ropes and looked at the ribbon lying by the fire.

'There's a funny thing, it's turned blue,' Eli said. 'No matter. I want you both to see for yourself what the flames can do to it. And count your last minutes,' he said, dragging Jacob and me forward.

He threw the ribbon of time onto the fire and started to count. The ribbon rose and ringed very slowly in a forward motion over the fire. When Eli reached the count of three, the fire went out with a sigh.

Eli reached for the ribbon with both hands.

Then he looked back at the fire burning fiercely, joyfully once more.

Eli looked from fire to ribbon in his hands, and then he started to scream.

'My hands, my hands, my poor hands. Look boy.'

I couldn't see any damage except that his hands were gnarling up, his fingers slowly bending inwards.

'Oh,' he moaned in a cracking, old voice as he handed me the ribbon, 'take the cursed thing.'

He shuffled towards me with his arms stretched out like an old man.

'What's happening to me?' he cried. 'Give me

some support, boy,' and then he toppled over.

'The ribbon ringed the fire three times, three times for the three ages of man,' Jacob whispered.

'Time and fire is the dragon's breath, it destroys,' I cried.

'You must make your peace with God, Eli, before it's too late or you will be damned for evermore.'

'Cut me loose,' Jacob cried. 'He is in extremis and needs a priest. Look! Eli is getting older all the time.'

And so he was.

His dark beard and hair grew long and grey and his eyes became watery.

'Where will we get a priest from in time?' I asked Jacob.

'Is that two boys I see before me, eh?' he mumbled through his toothless mouth. 'Come closer. What are you doing here? You put me in mind of two boys I had a wish to torment a long, long, time ago.'

'Why, Eli?'

'Why what?'

Jacob and I looked at each other.

'Do you repent, Eli?' Jacob asked him.

'I do that.'

'How do you feel when you repent?'

Eli's beard and hair were white and straggly now.

'I feel sorry like.'

His breath rattled in his throat.

'If you repent your sins I will make the sign of the cross over you,' Jacob said. He put some water on his hands and touched Eli's forehead with shaking fingers.

'It should be holy oil,' Jacob said. 'We'll soon see if water works. If it doesn't, he'll just disintegrate. Let's pray for his soul.'

147

We knelt down and prayed until Eli sighed his last sigh, then we closed his eyes.

When we looked down at him he looked at peace, an old man we might have met in life and never been afraid of.

'What power that ribbon has,' Jacob said in awe. 'Did you notice how it ringed forward to speed up time? What would happen if we made it go backwards?'

A sharp hiss rent the air, the fire flared up blue; Morgan le Fey was present..

There was something I had to remember, but what?

The hiss now rending the air was sharper than a knife; Morgan le Fey was getting impatient.

'It would be chaos,' I finally whispered. 'Forward is the way of time and fire.'

'Maybe you're right, maybe you're not. Supposing I turned the ribbon the other way over the fire just once to see what happens?'

'Why?'

'I was damaged before I was born when my mother went riding and was thrown by her horse. Would it really hurt if we put the ribbon over the fire and turned time back and stopped just before I was born?'

Do not turn back the dragon's breath
Time and fire bring certain death.

'Supposing your mother dies? You would be mother-less and you wouldn't have any sisters.'

Jacob crossed himself

'You're right. We are expecting another child very shortly. I have to protect my family in my father's stead, but this power is just so awesome, so tempting. I might not be able to stop pestering you to do it.'

He accepted that the power was conducted through me, but what would I say if he asked me where this power came from? I thought as I crawled out after him out of the hut. Time for that later.

First we had to free Boy, muzzled and tied to a tree.

'Did you see your crutches. Eli did take them.'

'The crutches? I don't need them now. I'm perfectly happy with a walking stick. I can't think why I ever made such a fuss about it. Being without arms is so much worse.'

Everything had changed, Jacob said as we got some feeling back into our cramped bones. He was happy now that he could cope, as happy as anybody could be who had his face bashed in.

'But you know what I'm like, Matthew. After a while I'll get grumpy and then I shall want to try and turn that ribbon back to that time before I was born.'

There laid the danger.

'So I will remove temptation. I release you from your promise to stay here until my father returns. You can go back home now Eli is no longer a danger. You can also take Percival.'

'Percival? The horse?'

'No, the knight from Camelot.'

It was wonderful. I would be going back to Horringer and be the blacksmith's boy once more. But how could I look after a horse, exercise it and feed it? We had enough trouble keeping ourselves warm and fed.

'Never thought of it,' Jacob said. 'But I just can't imagine not living with stables and servants to keep us going.'

I could, and then I wondered what people would say when they saw the great age of the dead who had kidnapped us.

'What is the matter with you? Eli died, that's all,' Jacob said. 'Maybe his heart gave out, but he wasn't old. About thirty, I should say.'

I crawled back into the hut and took another look at Eli. In life he had looked tormented, but he looked peaceful in death. He also looked very old. Time only ever moved forward.

'I've released you from my promise and I know it's important that you leave, and soon,' Jacob said, scratching his head, when I came back. 'Can you perhaps remind me of the reason? I think the reason is blue, but that is just too silly.'

We started to make our way through the dark forest towards the hall. Jacob had already forgotten how Eli had been destroyed by time and fire, the dragon's breath, but maybe it would come back to him.

I had better leave soon.

We reached the edge of the wood.

A meadow lark rose from the ground and flew up into the first blue of the morning air. Boy ignored the bird, settling between Jacob and me sitting down, when we saw a rider galloping towards us in the distance.

'Look, there's Alec,' cried Jacob.

Boy was excited, he was trembling, licking our faces and turning from one to the other.

'Calm down, Boy, we're all safe now,' I urged him. 'You'll have to guide Alec back to Eli's hide-out.'

When he sighed and rested his head between his out-stretched paws, Jacob said he believed Boy understood every word we said.

'My mother used to say a sheep followed a conversation better than I did, and if a sheep can, so can Boy.'

We looked at each other, suppressing a giggle, as Alec got ever nearer.

'I expect Alec will soon find another stable lad but it'll be hard to tell Frog I'm leaving.'

'Time for another of his slap-my-forehead-moments, I expect,' said Jacob, and then we started to laugh. We could not stop. We rolled about on the grass, tears running down our faces when Alec rode up.

'I'm glad you two are enjoying yourselves,' he said. He reined the horse in and looked down his nose at us. 'Have you thought of your mother at all who was giving birth last night?'

'Look at your face. YOUR FACE! And you in my care!'

'It's not your fault, and we're just happy to be free,' Jacob said. 'We were kidnapped last night. I was knocked on the head and carted off in a sack and tied up all night. So was Matthew. It was that dead man you'll find in the hut, Boy will show you. We freed ourselves, but please do not inform my father.'

'It's my duty, Jacob,' Alec said.

Jacob stood up. His blue eyes were blazing.

'That is an order! You are my tutor and therefore my servant. You will obey me! Are my mother and the child well?'

'Your mother has given birth to a healthy boy and she is well.'

'This is wonderful news. As for Matthew, I have given him leave to return to Horringer.'

When he told Alec there was a dead man to see to, Boy rose slowly and limped off into the woods once more, followed by Alec.

That's how it was. Alec had wanted Jacob to grow up, and now he had and he acted like a man, he didn't like it, Jacob said. 'Now why exactly did I release you from my promise? I can cope now, but it'll be a lot easier for me now I have a brother. The line will be more secure and the heat will be off me.'

I hadn't known that Lady Isabel had been carrying a child, but there again, why should I have been informed?

Jacob misread my silence.

'I expect you think I was getting above myself with Alec, but I was not.'

And Alec would take it, everybody liked to please Jacob, although not Gavin de Vere, who wanted to see Jacob fall flat on his face pulling an arrow. He came running towards us waving a bow when we finally reached the hall.

'Look Jacob,' he cried, the traitor, 'my best bow and arrow is for you,' but Jacob had his measure.

And no doubt you'd like to see me fall flat on my arse. And before you say anything, I can shoot from the saddle.'

'Hey, Gavin de Vere,' I shouted. 'Want to hear a riddle?'

He frowned.

'The last knight who was not, can be found
On the flatlands' chalky ground.
Do not turn back the dragon's breath.
Time and fire mean certain death.'

'What rubbish,' said Jacob.

He had truly forgotten *how* Eli had died, and he now had a brother. Jacob was *The Last Knight Who Was Not*, he had a brother, I thought. I had to be right, but there was no blue flash of light, and my heart didn't sing, whatever that meant.

It was time for me to leave, I said, but Jacob wouldn't hear of it.

'But you promised.'

'Are you implying I break my promises?' he said before he went off to play with his arrows.

Chapter 25

I was glad to go home and leave Jacob, but I was sad to leave Frog. He couldn't stand being cooped up, and there was also Martha.

'When are we leaving then?' he said - slapping his forehead as Jacob had predicted - when we met at the stables.

I had told him the tale about Eli, most of which he didn't understand, and about Jacob going back on his promise, which he did understand.

'We? Whatdoyoumean, WE? ' I said. 'Are you coming with me? How about Martha? And being cooped up in the smithy?'

'Martha? Her heart's set on becoming a nurse-maid. And it's *you* who's going to be the blacksmith's boy, not me. I'll find something else to do in Horringer.'

'You could look after sheep,' I said, 'they're outside.'

He rammed his hat on his head.

'I came here with nothing, and I have most of it left. Well, that's not quite true. I have a sixpence I never gave to my brothers and the clothes.'

I stared at him open-mouthed. He was coming with me! Then I started to cry. I could not stop. Then I collapsed.

Frog carried me to the stables where I fell onto the hay. When Boy crept in, I finally fell asleep, and I slept until cock-crow.

We left the hall a fortnight later.

I had only seen Jacob once, at Eli's burial. He shook my hand and wished me well, staring at the ground.

Not another change of mind!

'The thing is, Matthew,' he said, 'my mother absolutely refuses any further contact with you. She thinks you're dangerous. Things happen when you're about."

'I think she's right,' he added. 'Nobody thinks an old man like Eli could have carried you and me and the dog into the woods.'

'So that makes me dangerous?'

'You're hiding something. You have some sort of dangerous power I could wheedle out of you.'

'He'll make up his mind soon,' said Frog, when Jacob left.

The weather had finally broken.

Heavy rain drummed on the roof so Frog and I dressed in our working clothes. We would change into our best jackets and breeches before we reached Horringer and turn up on my doorstep looking like two fine boys.

Frog had changed since that day when Jacob had called him ugly. He walked upright now, and his eyes shone bright blue in his tanned face. His skin was no longer like tree bark.

'All that washing gives you a shine,' he said, smiling his crooked grin. 'I never reckoned it much before, well, never really until you came here.'

We packed our change of clothes into small bundles as well as the food cook had packed for our journey. We would be able to walk to Horringer in one day but Boy couldn't, so we would have to shelter somewhere overnight.

Unless we left him behind.

Boy was getting old. He was full of life, but now his muzzle was grey and his gait was stiffening. I told him with a heavy heart he could stay here. Somebody was bound to look after him, but he just rolled his eyes and trotted after us until I picked him up.

I suppose even he was longing to go home too, I told him.

'Too true, and don't hang about,' he said. Well, he just gave an angry, high-pitched yap, but that's what he meant.

Alec gave us a Florin each when we left the stables.

Frog said the money was our wages. I thought it was because Alec was glad to see the back of us, especially when he produced a couple of the large, waterproof capes - canvas boiled in linseed oil the grooms used for the horses - to cover ourselves with.

'What would you say if we didn't go after all?' I asked him, bundled up so only my nose and eyes were showing.

'Lord, lead me not into temptation,' he said. 'Clear off.'

We took the hint and walked off through the rain falling on us in torrents. We turned back before we turned left and took one final look at the hall. It sat massive, grey, with a secret life of its own behind the curtain of rain, the dark pines flanking it like guard dogs.

'What a dump!' said Frog.

I laughed. Jacob had hurt me, I had thought we were friends, but now I had my brother.

Night had fallen when we reached Clare, where I headed for the Austin Friar's. I wanted to tell Brother Aloysius that Eli had died peacefully, but Frog had other ideas.

'I have nothing against Brother Aloysius,' he said, slapping his forehead. 'But I could not put up with that other mad monk.'

Boy sat down and howled his blood-curdling protest.

'We could pay for their hospitality,' I suggested. 'I do have a Florin.'

'He's not getting his hands on that,' said Frog. 'He can have my sixpence.'

The meres around Clare were dangerously high. I wondered if they would flood again and hoped it wouldn't be tonight, with my luck.

Then I knocked on the door of the priory.

Brother Anselm gave us his usual warm welcome.

'Clear off!'

He had opened the door a crack, but Frog was wise to him; he put his boot firmly over the door step.

'How's your old bones?' I asked him, to be polite.

'Wass-it-got-to-do-wiv-you? I remember you. You should be hanged, you're horse thieves,' he said. 'Go away. I'll have no truck with horse thieves.'

He tried to shut the door.

'What do you want?' he asked when he couldn't.

'Hospitality for the night,' I said. 'Just shelter, and we can pay.'

'No eating,' he said, opening the door wider, 'and no admittance for that dog-creature.'

Boy sneaked in and shook himself vigorously. The rain fell off capes, leaving puddles on the floor while Frog searched for his sixpence. Brother Anselm bit into it before he scurried away.

'No. He's not eating it. He's making sure it's silver,' Frog said.

It must have been.

Before long, we sat silently warming ourselves in front of a fire burning brightly in a hearth, our stomachs rumbling.

'Keep the noise down,' Brother Anselm said. 'There are others in here asleep.'

He pointed to a few sleeping forms at the dark end of the room before he slunk off, slamming the door.

He was as mad as a cat sitting on hot ashes.

We waited as long as we could before we threaded the thick slices of bacon that cook had packed for us onto a poker and over the fire.

We jumped, still nervous when little blue sparks spat as the bacon grease fell into the fire in case they brought Brother Anselm scurrying back.

'How do you know these mad monks?' Frog asked.

I explained my mother, who was a famous beauty, had worked as a maid to a wool merchant in Clare. Her father and her three brothers had died of a fever, that's when she went back to Horringer.

'She wanted to be with her sister Elisabeth, Biddy,' I said. 'Biddy's mind turned to healing after the tragedy. She never married.'

So I was certain we would find my mother and father, Biddy and my grandmother when we would knock on our door the next day; two fine boys in the best clothes we intended to change into early the next morning.

But it's an uncertain world. It was still raining. After I had let Boy out I went back into the Priory's guest chamber, where I found Frog in the process of thanking Brother Anselm for something.

'Thank you,' he said, looking past the brother.

'Yes?'

'Thank you for...'

'I shall pass away before I know what it is you're thanking me for, boy,' Brother Anselm said.

'Hospitality, that's it. Look Matthew, that's the man who gave me the clothes.'

He pointed at a man sitting in a corner, lacing up his boots.

My father!

He didn't look up, and just for a moment I was tempted to sneak away. Why wasn't he at home like I had pictured it? What was he doing here, spoiling my homecoming?

He looked up.

When he saw us he didn't look in the least surprised. Relieved, but not surprised.

'You saved me a journey,' he said coming over. 'I was on my way to see you when the weather overtook me.'

It was as if I saw him for the first time. He had an air of authority. He was tall, with a jaw like an axe and a fine head of black hair.

'Any chance of breakfast for me and my two boys?' he asked. 'I have some news to impart, and it's best done on a full stomach.'

The life in Horringer Eli had described as 'going on just the same without me' had after all greatly changed. My grandmother had died, and my mother had given birth to a little girl, my father told us.

It was hard to take in.

I could not picture our cottage without my grandmother sitting around and talking to herself. And just as I had got to love having a big brother, I now had a little sister to get used to.

'Are they both well?' Frog asked, that seemed to be the right question.

My father said it had gone well. Her name was Elaine. My mother had these fancy ideas.

'Dare I ask what brings you two here?'

I told him Eli had died so it was safe to return.

'We've not been sacked. It's a long story I don't really understand,' Frog said. 'But we have a Florin each.'

Two Florins. Oh, the provisions that would buy

for the winter, my father said.

'The hens are egg-bound and the hedges are packed with berries, Biddy says, so it's going to be a hard winter, she reckons,' he added, holding out his hand for our money. 'Better the day, better the deed.'

'For going to market,' he added. 'In Bury St. Edmunds. I don't know any traders I can bargain with in Clare.'

We parted company by the old oak when we reached Horringer. My father borrowed my cape. He and Frog walked on to Bury while Boy and I turned and trudged through the village, past the blacksmith and towards our cottage.

It wasn't how I had visualised my homecoming. I had thought my brother would be beside me when I opened the door.

We stood there for a long time, Boy and I, watching my mother who was nursing the baby in my grandmother's chair, and Biddy, who was stirring a pot over the fire.

Boy moved first. He ran over to the chair and licked the baby's face.

'Don't stop the dog, Matthew,' Biddy said, turning round. 'He's making friends. He'll guard her from now on.'

My mother looked up and smiled.

'I expect you miss your grandmother, but she died very peacefully. She's with the angels now. I suppose the baby is a surprise for you.'

It was when my father told us over breakfast in Clare. 'They've gone on to Bury market.'

Biddy got up.

'Anything to get away. What's wrong with the market in Clare?'

She took the baby from my mother.

'Who exactly is "us"?' my mother asked. 'Is it

your brother?'

I wanted to tell them about Eli, but they seemed to have forgotten about him.

'What do you think of your sister?' Biddy asked proudly holding the bundle up for my inspection.

Not much. She had a screwed up little face and a pointed head.

'Now this is what I call a baby,' I said after some thought.

They seemed satisfied with that. Sometimes a big mouth can be an advantage.

Maybe Mattie would cheer me up, I thought as I ran down the village to the smithy, but she wasn't there.

'Gathering mushrooms afore they go off,' said the smith, wiping his hands on his apron. 'You're here then, boy. I can do with you.'

He had a man and a boy, I saw when I went into the smithy.

The boy wasn't much good, the smith said. He wouldn't last out the week. He had no idea that fire was a live thing.

'I don't get it, a live thing,' the boy said.

'Fire is like a boy, you might say. What has you and the fire got in common?'

I could almost hear Eli's voice again.

The boy kicked my shins. He would have to go. It was dangerous to get physical next to a large fire in the confines of the smithy.

'Hey, I'm talking to you,' he said.

'The fire needs air for burning,' I said. 'Eli told me that.'

'Oh?' the smith said. 'Is he still about? I thought he was long gone.'

160

He had died peacefully, I told him, and left it at that.

'We'll see you in the morning then,' the smith said, dismissing me. 'Unless you have a mind to take off again.'

What was the matter with me? All I had ever wanted was to return and become the blacksmith's boy. I was glad Mattie wasn't there to see my long face.

'Isn't this great,' whispered Frog that night as we laid in the dark, listening to the baby mewing like a kitten, the fire spitting feebly, Boy grinding his teeth.

Frog had wonderful plans for the cottage; porches to keep the rain off the door, lean-tos to keep the wood dry, filling the space under the cottage with straw to keep the floor warm.

'Are you starting on the work tonight?'

Frog gave it some thought.

'No. I have to be asked first. It's only polite.'

We started to giggle, and suddenly things fell into place, especially when Biddy threatened us with one of her famous brews if we didn't hold our noise.

It was great to be home, I thought, and then I started to worry about Mattie. Had Eli been right about 'her pretty ways' driving the boys mad?

Chapter 26

At first light I ran down the village to see Mattie, who I found yawning in the yard. She looked different, more grown up, wearing her hair piled on her head like a golden crown.

She was thirteen now, she said, that's why she had put her hair up.

'Is that what girls do when they are thirteen?'

She looked at me with her blue eyes.

'Is that what girls do?' I asked.

'It's *what I do*, silly,' she said.

'What are you like, you're making it up,' she cried when I told her Jacob and I had overpowered Eli after we had been kidnapped, I had an older brother called Frog and we had nearly been hanged as horse thieves.

'Some of it is true,' I said, 'Brother Anselm did think we were horse thieves. I was told your pretty ways drove the boys mad.'

'Pretty ways?' She stared at me. 'I don't have pretty ways, never had. They don't run in our family.'

'I have missed you though,' she added. I have had to pull the bucket up from the well myself,' she cried, flouncing off, seeing to the breakfast.

I put my fingers into my mouth and gave a sharp whistle, then we both looked up to the sky.

'No pigs flying there, shepherd's boy,' she cried.

I'm glad Mattie hasn't got any pretty ways, I said when I got home.

My father said what was the matter with me, Matilda was a fine girl, and he had two stupid boys on his hands, me and Jonathan.

'Who?' I asked, like the owl in woods. 'Who?'

'Oh, Frog,' I added. My father wouldn't hear of it and called him 'Boy', which brought the dog panting to his side. When he coughed to get Frog's attention, he had to drink one of Biddy's brews.

Now he called my brother Frog.

Frog had been a logger, so he knew the best places and prices of wood and charcoal for the blacksmith, and if a rider wanted a horse shod -which was rarely as only horses doing heavy work or carrying heavy loads needed to be shod- I ran for his help, he was so strong.

Life was good and peaceful.

'Peaceful?' my father said. 'A boy your age ought to yearn for adventure, not peace.'

Let somebody else venture out, I thought uneasily, there was my task to finish, and my mind turned towards the hall in Exning. Frog also wondered how Jacob was. If nobody came with some news about him and Sir William, one of us would have to brave the hall, we decided.

My father approved of us venturing forth like the hot-blooded youths we were not, but my mother did not.

'Whoever goes will be skinned alive by me,' Biddy said. 'I' wouldn't wish the worry we had when Matthew was away onto my worst enemy, if I had any.'

'At least Matthew has forgotten that nonsense about Camelot,' she later whispered to my mother, who crossed herself.

I worried about completing my set tasks and the riddles, and my father worried about Frog, about his appearance. His bearing was upright and there were no signs of the pock-marks of an early illness.

I was certain he would be off on his travels again, except for the weather; it was as cold as Biddy's hens had predicted, and the beginning was the worst.

When it snowed later, it was easy to think of it as a glistening blanket protecting the shoots in the silent earth.

The first sharp frost took us and the landscape by surprise.

Green fields and trees became a black wasteland overnight. Seagulls flew in from the sea on an icy east wind, screeching dire warning overhead.

'No use moaning about it,' Biddy said. 'Wrap up warm and don't go out unless you have to,' a sentiment pilgrims or travellers had taken to heart. Hardly anyone stayed overnight at the smithy.

The blacksmith's new man and boy had left shortly after my arrival. Village life didn't suit them and they didn't fit in the life of the household.

'I can do with you at dinner time, boy,' the blacksmith said. The company of women drove him mad, especially now that Poor Rosie never stopped chattering from one minute to the next.

I ate my dinner to keep company with the blacksmith who never said a word apart from 'Oh, aye, ahhr,' but when the blacksmith's wife's cry 'pots!' rang out, I bundled myself up and ran home until the weather became too cold.

'I can do with your brains if you got any, boy,' the blacksmith said one day, wiping his hands on his leather apron. 'I've had an order for iron railings and a gate. The top has to be in the shape of an 'A' but don't ask me why.'

The order would keep us going till spring, so I told him I knew my letters.

I fetched the slate and chalk my mother had used to teach me the alphabet and drew the "A", sitting at one end of the table.

At the other end, Mattie was making dough, Abigail was spinning, Poor Rosie wound the thread into hunks and the blacksmith's wife was by the fire stirring the potage.

We looked up when we heard a rider dismount and knock on the door of the smithy.

'He's got a black horse and black clothes and he's wearing black gloves and he looks like a boy,' Poor Rosie, who had answered the door, reported.

'Come in, come in. Now you look an educated sort of a man,' the smith said to Alec, for it was he.

'He is,' I said. 'He is Jacob's tutor. He'll tell you that letter is an "A".'

'Is it the boy or the letters you don't trust?' Alec asked just before I ran off to get Frog.

Boy left off guarding the baby from the fire and limped behind Frog and me to the smithy, where we found Alec and the smith discussing Eli's kidnapping of Jacob and me, and then Eli's death.

'What sort of man was Eli?' Alec asked.

'Good worker,' said the smith, 'as for character, if you asked him where he was coming from, he would tell you where he was going.'

'But he never went anywhere,' I cried.

'Aye, that helped,' he said.'

'I wouldn't have thought an old man like he was could have abducted the two boys in sacks, plus the dog,' Alec said, 'but the evidence was irrefutable.'

'Oh ahr, what you said,' said the smith, 'only Eli weren't that old, about thirty.'

'And yet the body was that of an extremely old man who wouldn't have been capable of blowing out a candle,' Alec said. 'There's the riddle. Can you enlighten me, Matthew?'

'I dare say Matthew could enlighten you if he knew what it meant,' the blacksmith's wife said from the depths of the room.

'What I want to say is that I feel I have nothing to tell you,' I said eventually. 'Except when Eli no longer was a danger to us he looked peaceful.'

'That's what Jacob said,' Alec sighed.

'How is Jacob?' Frog cried. 'We miss him and his weird ways.'

'Does he miss us?' I asked. 'Has Sir William returned from the war?'

Apparently, Sir William had come back from the war, but he had been wounded.

'Where?' the blacksmith said.

'In the side. He had a chink in his armour.'

'No, I mean where was he fighting?'

'In France. For King Edward and his right to the French throne,' Alec said.

'Right to the French throne?' the smith asked. 'Is that still going on?'

'He's still weak, I mean Sir William is,' Alec added, 'but the physicians think he will pull through. Jacob is well, but he will not leave his father for the present. Or his mother and his little brother. That's why he sent me.'

As he gathered his gloves, he pointed to the letters on the slate. His face was inscrutable and I wondered what was coming. Jacob had insulted him within my hearing, ordered him about, and called him a servant, and the smith had called him 'boy'.

Alec was proud. Would I become the scapegoat for his wounded pride?

'You can trust him with the letters, blacksmith, because you can trust the boy,' he said, but I didn't think he sounded convinced. Probably because he forced his words out as if they were sour apples.

The gust of cold air hanging around Alec left with him as he went out of the smithy.

The day was dark.

Flakes of snow danced around him when he mounted the horse.

He looked down at Boy, Frog, Mattie, Poor Rosie and me.

'I see you still got your retinue, Matthew,' he said, a smile hovering around his whiskered face.

Alec's heart was bigger than his pride. Not everybody was like Eli.

'And here is the present I was charged to deliver.'

He reached into his saddle bag and produced a sack full of chestnuts and walnuts to remember Jacob by when we roasted chestnuts and cracked walnuts around the fire at Christmas.

Frog and I talked about Jacob and the hall in the advent time heralding Christmas.

What a feast it would be with the boar's head and the musicians!

Although we would be happy enough to be warm and fed and in our own home decorated with holly and ivy, our minds turned towards Exning.

'Maybe,' I said, 'maybe...'

'Maybe nothing,' my mother said. 'Just for once I want everybody safely around me.'

And so we stayed.

We went to Mass on Christmas day. It was cold, the snow crunched underfoot, and our noses, sticking out from our bundled-clothes and hats, were red as holly berries.

On our return, we feasted on fresh bread made with just flour, not anything else my mother could lay her hands on, and sweet butter. We roasted chestnuts and cracked walnuts, and we ate in complete silence, cherishing every mouthful.

In the evening we went to the Manor, Elaine was fastened to my mother and kept warm under her coat.

We feasted on roast deer and meat pies and finished with a fine custard.

The fiddler played a jig, and I danced with Mattie.

Biddy laughed fit to burst. She said I looked like a cow on ice.

I have to admit I am not good at dancing, but my mother was right, there was nothing better than being with family and friends.

The time following Christmas was so bad that we needed something to hold onto because my father was taken ill.

He was so bad and evil-tempered, Biddy hid all the knives and Frog sat by his side, ready to do battle with him.

He had slipped on one of the frozen ruts in the ditch keeping the sheep out of the village. He was dazed and cold when Frog found him. His chest was sore, his head hurt badly and he could hardly bear the slightest noise.

That was the moment my baby sister chose to start crawling. When she made for the fire, Boy hauled her back and screamed fit to wake the dead.

My father was very poorly for a while.

After Biddy slapped poultices of hot pig's fat mixed with nettles onto his chest his breathing steadied, but he still knew nothing apart from an amazing amount of swear words and how much he hated us all.

'I shudder to think what poor little Elaine's first words will be,' my mother said to Biddy.

'If she's alive to tell the tale,' said Biddy.

After a while my father left off swearing. He started to recognise us and didn't mistake us for demons, but without any pleasure in us. He sat hunched over his plate at the table, jealously guarding his potage.

I was glad to escape to the smithy each day. The rest of the family - even Biddy - crept around in case he hadn't fully recovered his senses.

Frog asked if I had noticed how the cottage had shrunk under our father's bad moods.

After father had risen from his sickbed, my mother said it was a miracle. The miracle was that most of us still had our sanity and all our limbs, Biddy said, and it wasn't long before he announced he had a mind to go to trade in the waterproof capes for flour.

He looked around him to fend off the opposition but nobody was sorry to see him go, he was as bad-tempered as a man with his backside on fire and his face in a hornets' nest, but after he was gone we worried about him constantly.

He disappeared for some weeks and came back during Lent humping two bags of oatmeal. He dumped them on the floor in the outhouse, then he picked up his shepherd's crook.

'Time soon for the first spring lamb, I shouldn't wonder. Thomas the shepherd has been very patient with me.'

'Spring lamb?' said my mother, holding my pretty little sister up to him. 'How about us?'

'I'm truly sorry, Elena,' he said. 'I had to go away, I wasn't right in the head.'

I looked at my father standing in the doorway. He looked as tall, as handsome, as commanding a figure as ever, but there was a different look in his eyes.

'I had to go away, Matthew,' he said. 'Not because I wanted to this time but because I wasn't safe. I thought of harming all of you.'

'That makes a change from having itchy feet,' Biddy said after he left, 'but then if he hadn't, we would not have the blessing of Frog.'

'If you had seen your father when he strode first into the village,' my mother said, 'he looked like a knight of old, nothing like a simple cooper. My mind turned towards the Arthurian tales I had been told when I was a nurse-maid in Clare. The tales I told you.'

'I wished he would go away when he was ill,' I said.

'We all did,' my mother said. 'Why do you think we hid his knives?'

The smith had the last word on it.

'Oh, aye. Ahr. it happens.'

My father had also been an outsider most of his life and now he had become a villager, but why?

It might have been because he had been at death's door and he had recovered, or it might have been because he had brought some sacks of barley for the villagers.

I didn't know it then, but it would become very important later.

Chapter 27

It was well past Ascension Day when Brother Aloysius rode over to tell us Sir William had fully recovered his health.

The baby was now the prettiest little thing. A head full of shining blonde curls bounced around her little smiling face.

She had grown into her name; Elaine had pretty ways.

'And two teeth,' I said proudly.

'And she can talk,' Frog said. 'She calls me Ogg.'

'Isn't that just amazing,' Brother Aloysius said, 'I wish I could hold her for a moment but I can't, I've held too many sick people in this filthy habit.'

He got held up in the villages, he added. He would sleep in the blacksmith's stable and then ride on to Clare where he would clean himself.

At cock-crow, Frog and I ran down to the village where we found Brother Aloysius leading his horse from the smith's yard.

We walked with him for a little while. When the air struck cold and damp, his cowl became a hood covering his head. Now that it was milder, the cowl laid softly around his neck.

I looked at him closely, at his rolling gait, his bright sparrow eyes and his shining tonsure.

Then I asked him the question I had always wanted to ask.

'How do you keep your tonsure so shiny?'

'Questions, questions. What an odd boy you are.'

'If I don't ask questions, how will I ever grow up?'

'Slowly, I expect,' he said. 'If you must know,

we use pumice stones, but don't ask me where they come from.'

He started to laugh, his belly wobbling beneath his habit.

'But it does your heart good to laugh when laughter seems so hidden from the soul.'

'Talk about doing your heart good, how is that mad monk?' Frog asked the brother.

'Brother Anselm? He's just the same. A martyr to the world.'

That was not the word I would have chosen, I would have said a martyr to horse thieves, and downright unhelpful, I said.

'He helps those in need,' the brother added, 'and you never looked starved or destitute, Matthew.'

I thought again of our journey to Clare through the wintry wasteland, when I noticed the oak at the end of the village had sprouted newly greened leaves. The air was filled with birdsong and the scent of May blossoms.

There was always a gap. Easter followed Good Friday. Spring followed winter, light swallowed darkness, nothing could come of nothing.

My spirits began to lift, and then I saw it, laying in a clump of leaves beside the old oak.

A dead rat.

Although the rat wasn't particularly big it was black and covered in fleas.

'Nasty things, especially these new black ones,' Frog said, kicking it to make sure it was dead.

'Where do they come from?'

From the ports, Brother Aloysius said, the same as the smith had said when I asked him.

'Why are they so partial to ports?' I asked.

I thought the brother would say 'questions, questions,' but he didn't. His face grew serious.

'Rats get onto ships in foreign lands. They jump off the ships here and venture further, like the fleas they carry,' he said. 'The waters are travelled far and wide to bring back silk, jewels and gold.'

And sweet wines like the Claret, the grapes and spices for those who could afford them, I said, thinking of the hall in Exning and the grapes of the Blessed Abbot.

'There is something else you wanted to tell us when you came here apart from Sir William's recovery,' I said looking up at the brother sitting on his horse by the old oak, about to depart. 'Something you haven't told my mother and Biddy. It's to do with my father, isn't it.'

'Or with me,' said Frog. 'He isn't my father, is he?'

'No, he isn't.'

Apparently my father had returned to the family which had brought up Frog to give them the Florin Frog had earned where he had learned that the child, born out of wedlock, had some severe disfiguring disease of which it had died.

'But your father is proud of what he now considers his two sons, bloodline or not,' Brother Aloysius added. 'He told me so.'

He held his hand out and then blessed us with the sign of the Holy Trinity; the Father, the Son and the Holy Ghost.

'How can he be proud of his two sons when he's only got one?' Frog said after the brother had ridden from view.

I was never one for having a brother, but I've changed my mind.

'We'll become blood brothers. I'll cut both our thumbs and we say the words to make it important.'

'THE BROTHERHOOD.
   IN LIFE.
   IN DEATH.'

I said the words slowly, holding our two cut thumbs together, and our blood mingled.

Frog did the same.

'I knew you would think of something, you always have the words,' he said, but I didn't know where the words had come from, I knew only that they were right.

The wind rustled through the tree and the hairs on the nape of my neck rose as if I had stumbled across an answer to one of my tasks.

'*At last, but I have learned that time is a patient thing*,' a voice whispered in the wind.

I looked up and saw a blue light hovering in the crown of the tree.

'*Visit me here tonight*,' whispered Morgan, '*come alone. And make it an occasion.*'

Morgan Le Fey had commanded me.

Frog looked at my white face and misread my anxiety.

'You're right. I'm getting a real bad feeling about this dead thing myself,' he said, picking the dead rat up by the tail. He swung it over his head six times before he tossed it into the bushes.

Then we ran off and parted at the smithy where I met Mattie in the yard.

'Ouch,' I said, scratching and slapping myself madly.

'Fleas,' Mattie cried. 'You're crawling with the dratted things.'

She scratched her head.

Fleas and lice were generally not a problem.

They fell off us like ripe fruit when we covered ourselves and them with wood ash, and nobody was ever short of that.

'I refuse to go about all day covered in ash and look like an old woman,' Mattie said, 'and that is that. Let's wash them off at the stream. Abigail will have to perform a miracle and see to breakfast for a change.'

Frog was already at the stream, dunking his head in the water.

The water was clear, dancing over the pebbles, and it was shiveringly cold.

After we had washed the fleas off I tied my wet hair back with the ribbon into a ponytail and leaned forward to stare at our reflections in the water.

Mattie's hair gleamed red, like dancing flames, and from the water's midst's rose Jacob's pale face like a pale blossom.

'The thing is, Matthew, if you don't come soon you will be too late to see me again,' he said.

I rocked back on my heels.

I came to with a start and found Frog and Mattie staring at me.

'He does it quite a lot,' Frog said to Mattie, slapping his forehead. 'He stares into space until his eyeballs nearly fall out.'

'It's Jacob, he needs us,' I said.

'Are you sure?'

I leaned forward and looked into the flickering flames in the water again. This time I saw fires blazing from the ruins of the great hall.

'What do you see now?' Mattie asked.

'The hall. It's just a black shell. It's being eaten from the inside by a roaring great fire. And the barns are burning. And the horses are gone. We'll have to warn Jacob.'

'Maybe you're right,' Frog said, getting up.

'I do believe you saw something,' Mattie said.

'Why?'

'Your brown ribbon turned blue,' she said, raking her fingers through her wet hair. 'It turned blue when you stared into the water.'

The time had come.

Like it or not, I had to go, for someone, or something, was calling me to Exning.Someone, or something I was afraid off. Morgan le Fey would tell me tonight, but I would have to go alone.

'I'm going to Exning with Matthew and Frog tomorrow to visit Jacob, so I better pack some food for our journey,' Mattie informed her father later that day in the smithy, Frog and me by her side.

'I don't think so, my girl. Boys venture out, girls stay at home.'

'Why?'

'It's a dangerous world out there,' he said.

I said she would be perfectly safe, Frog and I would look after her.

'Where will she sleep, boy?'

He wiped his hands on his apron.

'In the barn,' said Frog.'

'In a barn? With all the men?'

'It's divided,' Frog said. 'One side is for women, the other for men.'

I kept my doubts to myself. Hadn't I seen the barn ablaze?

'If it wasn't for Matthew's worried look I might be more convinced it was safe,' the smith said. About to forge an axe head, he spat into the fire to gauge its heat. 'More pine and then the charcoal,' he said, wiping his hands on his leather apron. 'Let's go into the house and talk this over with the mistress.'

More than two or three words were always too

many for the smith, but not for the mistress.

'Never heard of such a thing in all my born days,' she said.

'But I want to go,' Mattie cried. 'I haven't been further than the village in all my life.'

'Neither have I,' said Abigail.

'And neither have I,' said the mistress, 'but I do have the good sense I was born with.'

'But not Abigail, didn't she fall down that there well?' the blacksmith said, a remark which Mattie interpreted not exactly as his blessing but as his approval.

It didn't go unnoticed by Abigail. She offered to comb out Mattie's' wet, tangled hair, with a less than saintly glint in her eyes.

'Best to avoid Bury St. Edmunds, boy,' the smith said later, back in the smithy.

The clear sound of the hammer on the anvil punctuated each word as his arm rose and fell. 'There's some kind of a mystery illness doing the rounds. Find out if it has spread to Clare and Exning.'

'Brother Aloysius didn't mention it. Apart from generally tending the sick.'

'Oh ahr, but he goes round villages, not towns. Our business comes mostly from the towns, boy. We haven't been what might be called busy just lately.'

If it wasn't the truth. The trickle of pilgrims and riders stopping the night had almost dried up. I wondered if it was to do with the new sickness.

Apparently it struck fast.

One way to tell the illness apart from an ordinary fever was by a swelling under the armpits.

'We will take care of your family if they need owt, boy, and if something were to happen to your father,' the smith said after supper that night.

Life was a kind of a queer thing, he said. Short

and uncertain.

His words were ringing in my ears as I ran through the village in the early evening light silently, distractedly, wondering how to tell my mother and Biddy that Frog and I were leaving for Exning the next day.

I knew my father would be all for us venturing out in the name of chivalry, whatever that was.

Quite a few villagers were still abroad that evening, standing in knots by their cottages, my father among them. He really was a villager now.

My mother looked worried when I told her we were heading for the hall tomorrow, but Biddy said it didn't come as a surprise to her.

'That's right,' Frog said. 'I already told her, I also told her I wasn't really one of the family.'

Frog was a blessing regardless according to my mother, and Biddy said if he was family he might not have turned out as well.

'Frog and I will only be gone for two or three days,' I said.

'That's what your father said once. You were about four when he went to market for some oatmeal. He was gone for over a year.'

'Just like his father, that boy. He can't stop in the same place for long,' I heard Biddy say that night as I waited for my father to come back from lambing and for sleep to overtake my family.

Except I was called to go, I was going to say, but I hesitated when my father came in quietly.

I waited until he had settled down, then I urged Boy to keep quiet. Silently and carefully I put on my best white shirt, made by my mother from the fine wool thread she had spun. I put on brown woollen breeches, black boots and a black leather jerkin.

When Morgan le Fey revealed my destiny under the old oak it would be an occasion, which meant best clothes.

I wore my best clothes but as it happened I never made it.

Chapter 28

I was up, fully dressed and ready to leave for my meeting with Morgan le Fey under the old oak tree, when the baby started to cry.

My mother sat up and stared at me in the darkness, faintly lit by glowing embers.

'Not yet, Matthew, it's too early,' she said cuddling the baby. 'Lay down and go back to sleep.'

I was only too pleased to do as I was told. I felt shivery and so itchy I couldn't stop scratching, my head felt as if something had come loose inside.

I waited until my mother had soothed Elaine, which took some time.

I'll go soon, I thought, soon, soon, but my eyelids became heavier and heavier and finally I fell into a deep, dreamless sleep. At least I could not remember any when Frog shook me.

It was morning.

My father's shepherd's crook was gone.

In its place were two rolled-up blankets.

'He said it was in case we didn't find any shelter overnight,' Frog explained.

'How do you feel?' I asked him when I came to.

'Thick,' he said, hunched over the table. 'Shivery. Itchy.'

'Where's Biddy?'

'Fetching the water,' my mother said, tying the baby to the chair and feeding her a spoonful of porridge. 'Don't worry. We still recognise water and wood when we see it.'

We donned our hats and coats when Biddy came back.

'Off with you,' she cried. 'Don't forget your blankets. Better the day, better the deed.'

When Boy howled she told him to be still. 'You

know you're not up to it.'

I looked back once. Elaine's mouth was wide open like a bird's waiting for the next spoonful. Boy sat at her feet hoping for a spillage.

Let down by this lack of interest in our leaving, we ran down the village where we found Mattie waiting for us at the smithy.

She looked different this morning.

Her normally pale skin glowed and her blue eyes were dark. Was it excitement? I asked her.

'More like temper. Abigail cut my hair off,' she said, taking her shawl off. 'It was such a tangle and my head hurt and she was in such a foul mood.'

Her hair stuck up like tufts of grass around her face.

'Mother said I would be burned as a heretic, and Rosie said she'd never heard of such a thing in all her life,' she said.

Then she pulled her shawl close over her.

'I thought I would feel excited about leaving for Exning but if it wasn't for Abigail I would be in two minds about going,' she added. 'I feel as useless as a melted candle.'

We all did.

We practically walked along from memory, and we felt worse as the day wore on.

'I was supposed to meet Morgan le Fey under the old oak,' I said trudging along, 'but I fell asleep.'

'You do live in a dream world, Matthew,' Mattie said.

'Only some of the time.'

The sun was at its highest point when we sat down by the road-side. A robin sang in the branches of a holly tree, crickets chirped in the meadows, insects danced all around us. It was all so normal and yet it was all so peculiar.

I had never met anybody on the road before. Now not only one or two lone travellers but quite a few trudged along, as well as a couple of families carrying bundles. They passed us silently, with bowed heads.

'Where are you from?' Mattie cried to the last one.

They walked on, as if stopping and starting was too much of an effort.

'Clare,' a little girl tied to her father's back cried.

Her father turned round.

His face was full of swollen, black lumps.

'Don't go there. They have a lot of sickness. The brothers have opened a hospice, but it's beyond them.'

'Is it the new sickness?'

'What do you think?' he said sadly.

A little boy by his side broke free. His face and arms and hands were a terrible mess.

'I think it's the end of the world,' he said slowly, looking up at us, hands behind his back. Then he collapsed, as if the ground beneath his feet had been suddenly snatched from under him. His mother came and picked him up but we didn't look at her.

I recalled Elaine opening her mouth like a bird. Mattie thought of Rosie and how she made her laugh. Frog remembered my father's concern, leaving blankets for us.

We sat there for a long time, talking of home.

The shadows lengthened before we finally rose.

'Maybe we were not meant to warn Jacob,' Frog said.

Maybe. Maybe we had to get far away from our village to take our sickness with us. Maybe we just had to go on and face whatever we had to face.

Hunger didn't bother us but we could have

drunk the world dry. As night fell on us we finally found a stream.

After we had quenched our thirst and emptied our bodies from the awful fluxes, we made a fire in the hollow of an old tree root.

Frog needed help to blow onto the sparks wrought by his flints, but the dead leaves and dry twigs we had heaped up soon caught fire with our combined breaths.

We sat huddled under our blankets, supposedly watching the flames but we all secretly felt under our armpits for signs of a swelling.

I didn't say anything when I found one under each arm, nor did Mattie and Frog.

What was there to say?

'We are friends, aren't we?' Frog asked softly after a while.

'We are that,' said Mattie.

'Friends deserve the truth, don't they?'

Friends did deserve to be told the truth.

I found it difficult to say it out loud, it had fallen on us so fast, but it had to be done.

'We've all got it,' I said. 'And it sure is painful.'

Then we laid down on the soft grass.

Close together under our blankets, we looked up at the moon, a pale sickle in the sky with the evening star dancing attendance. We saw the same and we were alike. It was a great comfort to us.

I could not say how many days and nights we trudged on, maybe only one, or two, or three, but it did not matter. Maybe we wanted to get as far away from Horringer as we could, maybe something else drew us, but finally we realised we could not go on.

We had walked through the night only stopping to empty our bodies again from the awful flux. When morning broke, we sat down on an old oak trunk split into two and blackened by lighting.

We supported each other and made the Act of Contrition for we were losing the ground beneath our feet and we had reached the end of our road.

I looked about me. The land was flat, chalky, and then, in the distance, I saw the large ring of hawthorn awash with white May blossoms.

I had been here once before with Brother Aloysius.

'It's the grave of *The Last Knight who was not The Last Knight*,' I said slowly. 'Brother Aloysius said it was hard to find, but now I know you can't find it. It has to find you.'

'I can do without a grave just now,' Frog said. 'Let's all think of something more cheerful.'

I closed my eyes when I heard Mattie's sharp intake of breath.

'Look at that white tree,' she gasped, pointing to an apple tree leaning heavy with blossoms blooming next to us.

It wasn't any old apple tree, oh no. Mattie's white tree was a miracle. It hadn't been there a minute before. The gnarled trunk bore its delicate load against the deep blue sky like floating white clouds, and yet I saw each white blossom edged with the tiniest tinge of red in the clearest detail.

We forgot everything, the past and the future, our pain; there was only a time of blossoms on a tree.

Then the tree started to change shape. But it was so slow a change that we did not see the transformation of blossoms into a magnificent white horse with a white mane wearing a white blanket, edged with red.

A tall but stooped old man with long white hair and a long grey beard, clad in a white shirt touching the ground, held its red halter in one hand. The other

184

clasped a black stick on which he leant.

'Did that please you, my children?' he asked in a deep voice.

We nodded.

'Then it was worthwhile,' he said. 'I wasn't at all sure if I ought to have wasted my strength on something that only brought a moment's delight. But that is my vanity, you see. I like my magic to be appreciated.'

'It was wonderful,' said Mattie. 'We forgot everything else.'

'All the pain, all the sadness,' I said.

'Ah yes,' the old man said. 'There will be pain and much sadness, but there will also be great joy. Morgan le Fey was going to foretell that to Matthew last night, but I stopped him from going. I had to, you see. I had to invade his dreams and show him the way here.'

'But I didn't have any dreams.'

'I merely erased your memory of them,' he said, leading the horse towards us.

I saw that the white horse's long forehead was divided by two lines, as in a cross.

'The cross shows the four phases of the moon,' the old man said when he saw me staring at it.

'Well, come on then. Up with you. Onto Swansdown. Swansdown is the name of the horse,' he said. 'I suppose it's not very original, but it was all I could think of in the spur of the moment.'

We stared up at him. We had to support each other just to sit on the old tree trunk. How on earth were we supposed to find the strength to mount a tall horse?

'Just think yourself onto the horse, my children,' he said. 'You have to help me a bit, you know. I can't do everything myself, apart from which, I have grown very old waiting for you.'

'How do I think myself on the horse?' Frog whispered to me.

'Picture yourself on it,' I said. 'You first, then Mattie and then me.'

We were sitting on Swansdown and riding off slowly before we knew it, looking at the old man leaning on his stick and guiding Swansdown I knew not where.

'I expect you are wondering who I am,' he said.

'I think you are a wizard,' Frog said.

'Of course, I think that would be obvious to a blind man,' he said. 'But I'm not any old wizard, I'll have you know. I am the last of the magicians. The last of the old magicians I should say for there will always be magicians even if they call themselves by another name.'

'You are Merlin,' I said, looking at his white robe, his domed forehead, his white hair and his beard, both finely plaited.

'You are Merlin the Druid. How about Morgan le Fey? You did say you were the last of the old magicians.'

Morgan was the last sorceress, Merlin said. 'She is a great sorceress. She makes charms of concealment, charms against burning so flames cannot touch her, as she did when she was in the flame at the burial of Eurith, the Strong. Do you know why she is so great, my children?'

He paused.

'Morgan le Fey *wanted to learn all about magic*. She hungered and thirsted for it. In other words she was eager for it. You have to be schooled in spells and enchantments, you have to be tried and tested and fail many, many times before you finally succeed.'

Nature had to be obeyed before it could be

controlled, he added.

'What does that tell you about nature? What do you think I mean by obeyed? Who *did you obey*?'

'I obeyed anybody,' Frog ventured. 'I had to. I got beaten otherwise.'

'I didn't,' Matilda said. 'I would never obey Abigail, but I obeyed my parents. They have lived longer and and they know better than me.'

'I obeyed the blacksmith and my family and Alec, but I would never obey Eli,' I said. 'I didn't respect him.'

'I knew we would come to it if I waited long enough. RESPECT!' Merlin shouted. For all his age he had a most marvellous, strong voice. 'That's the word I was after.'

I was still puzzled. Nature had to be respected. I had never thought about it but I had taken it for granted; you sowed in spring and reaped in autumn.

But how could nature be bent to transform a tree into a horse? I asked.

'You are a sharp one and no mistake. Changing a tree into a horse can't be done unless you understand that neither can live without the necessities of life.'

'Like a fire.'

'Just so, Matthew. When your brother made a fire in the hollow of the old tree root last night he used nature to make the spell of fire.'

He chuckled.

'Now, these new breed of magicians who call themselves alchemists don't always understand that. Some do, and some have great minds and discover new mysteries. Some are monks.'

He paused.

'They have the time for it. But there are also great minds, magicians by another name, in the school in that little fishing village by the river Cam. One of them, or it might have been a monk, ' Merlin said, and then he stopped for a laugh which sounded like distantly rumbling thunder. 'One of them tried to transform base metal into gold and blew himself up into a thousand pieces.'

The horse neighed, and Merlin looked at him.

'Swansdown wants me to show you something.'

He let go of the reins.

'I am left-handed,' he said. 'I believe it's called sinister, but then all wizards are.'

'Sinister or left-handed?'

'Work it out for yourself, Matthew.'

He closed his eyes, pointed his stick which turned into a wand and cried out in a loud voice.

A fresh oak leaf landed on his outstretched right palm.

'WATCH!'

Merlin mumbled something under his beard again, and before our amazed eyes the leaf turned into slippery green-scaled fish.

'I have made a fish in respect for you and your religion,' Merlin said. 'For some incomprehensible reason a fish is also a symbol of Christianity.'

When the fish started to gasp for air he shut his eyes again and the fish turned back into an oak leaf.

'I saw it,' I cried.

'So did I,' cried Frog. 'I saw right into it. The skeleton of the leaf and the fish are exactly the same.'

Merlin opened his eyes.

'What else did you see?'

'You pointed with your wand,' Mattie cried.

'That's right. You have to *project* your will along the wand towards the object.'

'So it's no use just calling to it.'

He leaned on his stick and we started to move again.

'Just so,' he said. 'But I did not have time to change the tree into a horse.'

He could have done it with magic mushrooms and sacrifices - oh yes, nature demanded sacrifices - and a full moon at midnight.

If I had had the time for it of course, which he did not have.

'You made us all picture the same thing at the same time,' Mattie said.

'Frog said let's think of something more cheerful, but I didn't think of a tree,' I said.

'But you all cleared your mind and I was able to plant the image of a tree in your mind,' Merlin said. 'And maybe you think "what an old fraud that Merlin is," but it is far from easy to plant the same image at the same time into three very different er...thought processes.'

He was a true magician, Mattie cried. He looked and acted like one.

'If it looks like a duck and quacks like a duck and waddles like a duck I shall call it a duck,' she cried.

The secret strength of the mind had all been ignored and forgotten.

'Now in Antiquity,' he added, 'it is rumoured that at the time of the dragons and building of the great stone henges that our ancestors knew how to transport matter through thought, although I believe they used teams of twelve oxen. My feelings tell me it is so, but I have not travelled back in time to observe it.'

'Going back in time is far too dangerous,' I cried.

'Just so. Forgetfulness is dangerous, but so is dreaming backwards. I cannot *prove* that matter can be transported by thought, but I have heard tales that the Christian Faith can move mountains,' Merlin said. 'I haven't any evidence of it either, of course, but I saw how your religion's ritual cut off the flow of time.'

'You mean what Jacob and I did with Eli to stop him disintegrating?'

Merlin nodded.

'But Swansdown reminds me that I must come to Matthew and to his tasks, but it is a good few hundred years since I last had a decent conversation and I do so enjoy talking.'

He glanced at me with grey, wise, hooded eyes.

'Well? Why don't you ask the questions now that they can be answered?'

There was so much I wanted to ask and so little time.

'*The last knight, who was not, is to be found on the flatlands' chalky ground,*' I said. 'I thought that I had found his grave, and then I thought it might be Jacob, but who exactly is he? And who is the First Knight who was not?'

Chapter 29

'He is Eurith the Strong. He is a descendant of the true first knight, Lancelot, who was *The First Knight*. Eurith worshipped the Germanic God Wotan. So he was buried with his horse and shield for use in the afterlife.'

'The religion complicates everything,' I said.

Merlin laughed.

'Religion is the most divisive force on earth. But I do not want to talk of bloodshed, I've seen enough of it to last me untold lifetimes.'

He gestured with his staff as if he was parrying blows.

'I've had my fill of chopping off limbs and slicing through bodies and cutting up livers. Perhaps it is not generally known, but I am not only a great wizard but I was also a mighty warrior.'

He had fought for King Arthur of the Britons, he added. The king was the nation, that would never change.

'I digress, I digress. It is my vanity again, you see, I do so like to be admired.'

He sighed.

'But why did you bring me to the hall?'

'Understand this, Matthew. I did not bring you to the grave. It found you when you went to the hall where you found a brother even if he was not of your line.'

'And then Frog and I had sworn an oath of allegiance to each other under the old oak.

> *THE BROTHERHOOD.*
> *IN LIFE.*
> *IN DEATH.*'

'Just so,' said Merlin. 'You, Matthew, voiced the motto

of The Knights Of The Round Table. You were chosen to be the Seeker.'

'Some 'Seeker'. Full of disgusting bumps and leaking lesions and a leaking body.'

Merlin reined the horse in abruptly. He held up his stick to heaven and closed his eyes and before we knew it we were asleep.

Merlin laid on the ground when we woke up, or rather he seemed to be part of it. You could not tell where one started and the other finished apart from his nose sticking up into the air like a well-used, bent kitchen knife.

He rose slowly, wincing and sighing as if he was in pain.

'Coming to does hurt so, and then it tingles but I don't mind that,' he said.

'Like when your hands warm up after they froze?' Mattie asked.

He nodded, and we set off again.

'I have removed the outer signs of your illness during your sleep,' he said. 'I cannot cancel your sickness, of course, it would mean going back in time, but you are good children and I want you to be beautiful.'

I looked at my hands and arms, now clear of the poisonous swellings. Frog and Mattie were clear as well according to their gasps of delight, for of course, I was sitting behind them.

'While I was at it,' he said, 'I made Matilda's hair grow and I wove some cornflowers into it. I thought it might please her.'

Merlin was indeed a great wizard, I thought as I looked at Mattie's hair sparkling like flames before me.

The horse started a slow canter, and then Mattie asked the question that mattered.

'What have the Knights of the Round Table got

to do with Matthew?'

'It has to do with *"The Last Knight, who was not the last"*,' I said. 'Just who is he? Have I met him?'

'You have, Matthew. Your father is not the last descendant of Lancelot.'

'Because I am,' I cried.

I remembered my mother seeing my father as a knight in shining armour when they met. I remembered his disgust at my lack of spirit, of chivalry, because I liked being at home.

Merlin must have read my thoughts, for he said my father had been wrong.

'You looked after Jacob in the woods? And didn't you put Matilda between your brother and yourself so she would be supported?'

That was the true meaning of chivalry, Merlin said.

So I was a descendant of Lancelot.

'You are not The Last Knight who was not,' said Merlin. 'There has to be joy and also sadness.'

'Did our families get the plague?' I asked.

Merlin shook his head. He had looked into the future when he was weaving his dreams.

'Your village was spared because you ventured out and took the sickness away from them. But your family's grief,' Merlin said, 'never went away entirely, even if your parents had another boy, that was a joy. How could sadness go away? Three children lost is a great tragedy, and they blamed themselves for letting you go so easily.'

'It was as if a shroud covered the village. Villagers hobbled about bent over like old people. The children whispered and your dog howled night and day,' he said.

He shook his head at the memory.

'But then it was thought you three were buried

193

with the other plague victims of Exning. You recall the little boy you met at the wayside? If you had looked at his mother you might have seen that the disease didn't affect her. Some people are immune to it.'

The plague, he said, spread not by the rats but by their fleas, had spared the little boy's mother. She had reported seeing us sitting by the wayside but they never found any signs of us.

'Are you sure about all this?' Frog asked Merlin.

He laughed.

'I might have turned you into an earthworm once upon a time for your impertinence. I always think there is no worse existence than that lead by an earthworm. Very unexciting. That would show you.'

'Biddy always said my father had itchy feet,' I said.

Merlin shook his head.

'We sent your father on his journey to find his son, a brother for you. He found a blood brother, and you swore allegiance to each other, uttering the name of the brotherhood.

'Just a minute, let me get this straight,' cried Mattie. 'If Matthew's father was a descendant of Lancelot but he was not the last, and if they had another boy, what does it mean?'

'Where do you think you are now, Matthew?' Merlin asked.

'*On the flatlands' chalky ground*. I am the last knight who was not the last on this ground.'

'Matthew is a descendant of Lancelot,' said Mattie. 'And if his father had another boy, it means he won't survive this illness. All three of us won't.'

'What a sorceress you would have made,' cried Merlin.

He added that we hadn't asked yet where he

was taking us but he would tell us just the same.

'You three will go to *Neitherland*. You will reside there until a new legend is born, one who will make the land bloom. Matthew will release the spirit of the First Knight Who Was Not The First Knight and lead you all into the "Hereafter" where you will find everybody who you have ever loved.'

He turned to me.

'BUT BE WARNED,' Merlin added, pointing his wand at me. 'DO NOT LET YOURSELF BE DISTRACTED. BEWARE THE NIGHT OF THE FLYING SPOOKS.'

Merlin lowered his wand.

'But first I will lead you to a place where the ancient ley-lines dividing the country since Antiquity cross, for it is at their crossing-point that magical events can occur.'

'I don't understand this at all,' Mattie said. 'All this about flying spooks and finding knights who are not. Wouldn't it be much easier to find people who are?'

'I think it would be a lot easier,' ventured Frog. 'And what if Matthew forgets all those things you just said?'

'Nobody had promised it would be easy, and forgetfulness was a dangerous thing, very dangerous,' Merlin said again, waving his wand at me.

If we didn't know where we were coming from, how could we possibly know where we were going and who we were?' he asked us. 'To put it simply, what good is a man who loses his memory?'

I thought about it.

'I expect he would have to reinvent himself, just say he is somebody else,' said Mattie. 'Simple.'

'What if he has no imagination?' countered Merlin.

'He would die with the sheer terror of it all,' she said.

Merlin shot her a glance of the purest adoration.

'What a mind,' he said, 'and what a sorceress I could have made of you at one time.'

He shook his head again.

'No matter. I now have to take you to the place where the energy lines cross, as I have said, in case you have forgotten it already.'

'I'll do my best to take you there but my power is not what it was. My power is that of the old Gods and you know what happened to them?'

'Not really,' I said. 'For instance, what happened to the Druids?'

'The Druid priests were singers of songs and weavers of dreams and they charted the movement of the heavens. But the people grew careless of their good fortune. So the great God Lug threw his mighty hammer onto the earth and brought darkness onto the land to frighten the people into turning back to the Druids.

'The wasteland!' I cried. 'But it didn't work.'

'Alas, no,' Merlin said. 'The plagues and starvation the darkness brought onto the land made Arthur and his Britons turn to the new God the invaders from across the sea believed in, the same God of the one called Padraig who drove the snakes from his island, the God of the true Faith as he is called. The Druids faded because they had not reckoned on the consequences.'

We were patient to put up with his ramblings about the old times, he added, even if we had no choice but to listen. But then we were good children. We had a shining humanity.

I wasn't too sure.

'I'm proud,' I said. 'I think I'm indispensable.'

'I'm nasty,' Mattie said. 'I want everybody to obey me.'

'I'm stupid,' said Frog. 'I can't think for myself.'

'So name our shining humanity,' I commanded Merlin.

He smiled.

'I will name it,' he said, 'for by naming things we can recognise them. Your shining humanity is your wise use of the life force.'

He paused.

'Picture the life force as having many connections, like a spider's web. Yes, that's it. A spider's web. Just like a spider's web the life force sends out vibrations for good or ill, and you used your energy to care for others.'

He invaded our minds once more and we fell asleep.

He had shrunk, and he looked weary when we woke up.

'What will happen to you, Merlin?' Mattie asked.

'I will join the bright regions of *Eitherland* in the wide blue yonder,' he said, pointing to the sky above.

'Is that what Druids do?' Frog asked.

'It is what I, Merlin, the last of the old magicians and the greatest wizard of all will do to celebrate my death. I have chosen this way of nature when I go to the *Isles of the Blessed*.'

'Do they exist only if you believe in them?'

He laughed a dry laugh.

'You are right, and also wrong. The Isles exist, of course, but going to *Eitherland* will make me find them. And then I will pass on again. We are part of nature and nature constantly renews itself, it is the ring of nature as recorded in the great stone henges. But first I will have a Druid's end.'

He added that a Druid's body was burned.

'I am dying peacefully now, but I know somebody who is willing to burn me when I'm dead. I will join the hall and the barns set aflame as you foresaw in the village stream, Matthew. The flames will purge the land from the plague.'

'How about Jacob? What will happen to him? Where will he go?'

'Jacob and his family have fled with their servants and they are safe even now,' Merlin said. 'Jacob is young but his destiny has been made clear to me. He has already made up his mind to wed one of the nurse maids, against fierce opposition, I might add. I forget her name, but she had an open look in her eyes.'

'Not Martha,' cried Frog.

'I believe that is her name. She is of greater years but she is a pleasant girl of great compassion and capable of much love.'

'What was the name of the scribe, tutor, whatever?' Merlin continued. 'The pale one who had the look of a clever child about him?

'Alec,' Frog and I cried.

'Yes, Alec.'

He paused.

'He became a wanderer looking for the lost children. He refused to believe you were dead, you see. He fetched your dog, Boy, who stopped howling, and he and the dog roamed the land.'

'Alec? But why?'

'He loved you and your brother, and he did not have the responsibilities of the blacksmith,' Merlin said. 'And your father, Matthew, would not leave his family. Not ever.'

'But Boy was old,' Frog said, 'and his bones

hurt.'

'Just so,' Merlin said. 'But Alec carried him in a sling in front of his chest. Alec's beard grew long and it was hard to tell where his beard ended and the dog started.'

I was going to ask him about Brother Aloysius when I noticed that Merlin wasn't too pleased our attention had turned away from him.

The horse stopped and we got off in a wild place of old oak trees forming a canopy overgrown with dangling strings of ivy.

We followed Merlin who held his wand straight out in front of him. The wand turned left and led us into a fragrant ring of elder bushes, their flat disks of cream blossoms held like lanterns towards us.

Finally Merlin's wand divined our resting place by an old yew.

'The ancient energy lines cross here because, long ago, a Druid Priest's ashes were buried in a hole over which a yew tree was planted.'

The wand pointed to the ground where white camomiles tilted their flower-heads to the sky and released their scent.

We laid down in the secret place where the ley-lines crossed, Mattie in the middle, clasping hands.

'I look forward to being one with the elements, to becoming ever-changing clouds for a while,' he said, leaning on his wand. Then he raised it to the sky. 'And I'll take great pleasure in bringing down sudden down-pours, sharp hailstones, great bolts of lightning striking like swiftly darting arrows, and enormous claps of thunder like a thousand wild horses to frighten those who deserve it,' he said.

'For a while, anyway,' he added.

We believed him even as we fell into a deep sleep.

Chapter 30

Edwin's place.

'And then I heard a boy,' I finished. 'He was crying. I thought it was Jacob.'

'But it was me,' Edwin cried.

It had taken some time before I came to the end. It wasn't only school and bedtimes which got slower and slower but also when I recalled my friends and my family.

We were in Edwin's bedchamber, Edwin, his grandmother, and I. His grandmother was busy knitting a garment for Edwin. She called it a jumper.

'Showtime!' Edwin cried, waving his notes above his head. 'Showtime!'

'That's right, Matthew,' his grandmother said. 'It's a saying we have. 'Let's get the show on the road! Izzy wizzy let's get busy, that sort of thing.'

Some sort of a spell.

Edwin sat down and looked at his notes.

'What it means is that we have a mystery here. And a proper mystery has a solution.'

He ran his hands through his blond hair and put his glasses on.

'And I AM NOT only hopeful but absolutely certain we can solve it. So let's go and GIVE IT SOME!'

He sighed.

'To be honest, I had hoped Jacob would be connected to The Last Knight who wasn't the last,' he added.

'But why? I am proud of being a descendant of Lancelot,' I said, although I hadn't got quite used to the idea yet.

'You should be proud to come from the

legendary Lancelot, well I assume he is,' he cried. 'Only I thought there might be a connection between me and Jacob. You know, we're both sons of warriors. And you found me by the yew at the magic place where the ley-lines of Antiquity cross.'

I thought about it.

'That might be so. I might also have been drawn to you because you are, like Jacob was, the son of a warrior, you are the son of a warrior who flew the clouds.'

Edwin looked pleased.

'And now you have to fulfil the last task and solve the riddle of Closing The Ring,' he added, looking at his notes.

'Perhaps you can read it out loud to remind me,' I said.

'To find the nobleman, who is not, I'll not give aid, but you, Matthew, will not be afraid.'

'Next,' I said.

'First follow your heart and make it sing. Look for three signs who have to be "other" to close the Ring.'

'These three signs have to be "other" which means they have to be different,' Edwin said.

'Next.'

I found it very easy to say 'Next.' If only everything else was as easy.

'The ribbon will bend - to find the answers - the questions will mend. Follow your heart and make it sing. For only joy can close the ring.'

'The ribbon which has to 'bend' ~is the ribbon of time, I should think, bends means connect,' Edwin said. 'So this part helps you to find the answers. The questions will mend ~means solving the riddle and return you to from where you came.

'But it's very hard to find answers if you don't

know the questions. It was awkward, like finding people "who are not".'

But the riddle was set by Morgan le Fey who was not only very awkward but extremely contrary, I said, 'she did give a clue, *bend to connect*.

Then I cried, 'Next', but there was no next.

'"Bending" might be like a loop,' Edwin's grandmother said looking down at her knitting. 'Like a stitch that has to be connected with the one below.'

I thought about it.

'Something from the present has to connect us to the past,' I suggested.

'And "your heart singing" probably means getting excited,' Edwin said.

'But before we jump up and down we have to find the present and the past,' said his grandmother.

Edwin might not like her *muscling in,* but she was a wise woman. Not a wise woman with herbs like Biddy had been who had used healing herbs like St John's Wort and who had avoided the poisonous Monks Hood. Her wisdom was more like that of Brother Aloysius, I said, but I was getting anxious about the date. I had to be gone by the time of All Souls Day.

Didn't Merlin say, 'BEWARE THE NIGHT OF THE FLYING SPOOK?'

'Halloween is on the thirty-first of October. My birthday is on the twenty-ninth but it isn't important for me this year,' said Edwin. 'I have had an exciting time listening to you.'

'It's nearly the end of August, we have a bit of time left.'

I will say one thing about Edwin's age, they always knew the exact date and time although I don't know what difference measuring time made to them.

'School for one thing, Matthew,' Edmund said glumly.

'What's going on in here?' Edwin's mother said, she had come in quietly, 'and Mother, why are you sitting in Edwin bedroom, knitting?'

We all looked at her as if she had no right to be here and, to no-one's surprise, she took to her heels and she fled.

To my surprise, it was a bright day, and it was already noon when we went into the kitchen.

Edwin's father came in, and he had a great presence, and also another boy, thin and dark-haired, who stood fidgeting in the doorway.

'We've fetched Jonathan for you, Edwin. He's at a loose end as well,' Edwin's mother said. 'You need some company apart from your grandmother. You're getting very odd.'

'I'm not at a loose end and I'm not getting odd,' said Edwin. 'It's just that I've got loads to do before Halloween.'

'I wasn't bored either,' Jonathan said sulkily. 'It's my parents. I like playing on my computer and they think I need fresh air.'

After they had eaten some flat thing with something red and disgusting called tomatoes on top, the boys left, muttering it wasn't their fault if the air in the house wasn't fresh. They were going on 'the rec' to play football.

Edwin had explained to me it was called football because the ball was kicked by a foot, and when it touched their heads it was called 'a header'.

What else? I thought.

Edwin's grandmother went to 'the hairdresser', dresses for hair, whatever next!.

In the quiet descending onto the house, Edwin's parents found themselves lost for words. As Edwin's father washed the dishes, his mother dried them in polite silence.

Then she picked up a book and dark glasses and wandered to the bottom of the garden.

She tried to get into a stringy thing slung between two trees. It flipped over and flung her to the ground.

She looked suspiciously towards the house to see if anyone had witnessed her humiliating downfall before she tried again.

The thing swung alarmingly.

She steadied it and her glasses fell off her nose.

She put them back on.

It swung again and her book fell to the ground; I could stand it no longer.

I steadied her. Then I picked up her book and put it into her hands.

'Thank you,' she said automatically.

Then she said 'Oh, my God', several times.

She couldn't see me, and it appeared to put her out of sorts every bit as it did me. I do not like being ignored. I am not used to it, but if you are invisible that is what happens.

By settling Edwin's mother I hadn't been able to see his father, but I shuddered when I saw he was getting a very old and rickety wooden ladder out of a hut.

'I do hope you're not thinking of going up on that thing, Earl,' Edwin's mother cried. 'You know you've not got a head for heights.'

I was surprised to hear it. He had flown in the air and ridden the clouds and yet he did not like standing on a ladder, fixed to the ground?

'I'll be all right,' he said, humping the ladder to the house. 'The gutter's blocked.'

He extended the ladder and put it against the wall, but not before I had seen that the two top rungs were missing.

'Make me a cup of coffee first, would you?' Edwin's mother cried. 'My nerves are shot to pieces.'

While he was indoors busying himself with the boiling water - a ruse to keep him on the ground - I removed the ladder from the wall and put it back on the ground.

When he returned, he looked at it and scratched his head. Then he set light to one of the twigs. When it was burned out, he put the ladder back against the wall.

Then a shrill noise from the house demanded his presence. I had heard this mysterious summons many times before, and I took the chance to put the ladder back on the ground. Alas, I could not stop him from climbing it when he came out again.

'Aha, a tennis ball,' he said, stretching to his right and taking his right foot off the rung. The ladder wobbled.

He tried to put his foot back on one of the missing rungs.

He fell off.

I was glad I was able to catch him. While I was at it, I turned him back on his feet before he touched the ground. It's so undignified to lay on your back waving your legs like an upturned beetle, especially for a man like Edwin's father. He was so tall, with such a good, handsome face.

I turned round when I heard what seemed to be an animal screaming in pain. It was Edwin's mother who unwound herself from the stringy thing between the trees and ran towards him.

'Oh, Earl. Darling, I thought you were going to fall off the ladder and I'd lose you again. I couldn't bear it!'

'There, there, Jennifer,' he said.

I left them. I had no wish to spy on them in their happiness on finding each other again, and I also heard a cart disturbing the gravel in front of the house.

Edwin's grandmother, who wore no dresses on her hair, and the two boys got out.

'Found them loitering by the ice cream van with intent,' she said over my shoulder to Edwin's parents.

'Within tent!' cried Edwin, and the two boys laughed fit to bust.

'Talking of odd,' she said looking at the boys, 'I'm going home shortly. Don't look so pleased, Earl, I'm coming back. Get your things, Edwin, and don't forget your notes. We'll drop your friend on the way.'

'My father's picking me up,' said Jonathan.

'All the better', she said as we got into the cart or car, as it is called now.

Chapter 31

I don't know which was worse, the noise or the speed at which we travelled along the wide road. All the other cars also simply whizzed by us. Some of the others - as big as houses - travelled either in front or behind us or even worse, headed straight for us.

'I'm surprised with that sort of speed the car does not take off and fly in the manner of a bird,' I said.

Edwin's grandmother said she herself was constantly amazed herself that aeroplanes could fly and cars could not.'Edwin's grandfather knows about such things. I'm not educated in that fashion myself.'

She drove on for some time, finally stopping in front of a red brick-built house in a row of identical houses.

'Grandma's house has a blue front-door,' Edwin said to me. 'You like blue. You know, the blue of the heart of the flame.'

'Fire is either red, yellow or orange, and B&Q are unlikely to stock paint called blue-of-the-heart-of-the-flame,' she said. 'This shade is called "*Bluebell Surprise*". The surprise was the wishy-washy blue.'

The blue-at-the-heart-of-the-flame. For some reason I relived the scene where Edwin's parents had resolved their differences. But what was the connection? Was there something of significance behind that blue door? Or was it the journey that I had mostly disengaged myself from?

There was nothing disturbing about Edwin's grandfather who came in shortly after we had washed up dishes and cutlery probably worth a king's ransom, there was so much of it.

He was a small, kindly man with an intelligent

face under a frizzy red tonsure. He had a lively look about him.

'Ah, Edwin,' he said to the boy. 'I believe you've grown.' He seemed surprised.

He turned to the boy's grandmother. 'I didn't expect you back so soon, Violet,' he said, before he disappeared into a hut down the bottom of the garden.

'He's a civil servant,' Edwin's grandmother said.

'I should hope so. Servants have to be civil,' I said, 'or else they catch it.'.

She gave me a thoughtful look and said we had no time for lengthy explanations.

Edwin's grandfather went to work in the morning, returned in the evening, when he ate his dinner, and then he mostly disappeared into his shed where he was turning, Edwin said..

I had heard of turning in bed, but never before of turning in a shed, but it was a strange age.

'He makes things out of wood, my grandparents don't have a television,' Edwin said. 'They listen to the radio, which suits me. I want to keep my mind clear.'

Television. Radio. More of these words I had come to disregard. I had to, really, and concentrate or I would miss my cut-off date -as Edwin called it- of Halloween.'

They knew the exact time and date, but some things they tried to make wise to me were totally unbelievable, like for instance *making the weather*.

I found this out the next day.

We were driving along the road in the morning back to Edwin's house, when Edwin's grandmother switched on a voice she called a 'radio' in the car.

'For the weather forecast,' she said.

I had to laugh. Nobody can make the weather.

'A high is moving in from the south,' a voice

told us. 'There will be a few scattered showers in the east which will die out in the night.'

'What does it mean?' I asked. 'What are these highs?'

'The opposite of lows,' Edwin's grandmother said. 'One brings rain and the other doesn't.'

She shook her head.

'I'll not go on the by-pass,' she said. 'Apparently there's been a spillage and there are tailbacks so I'll go through Newmarket.'

'You might like Newmarket. It's famous for its horses,' Edwin said. 'In fact Newmarket is the home of horse racing. Well, you like horses and used to work in stables.'

I sat up. I felt a rising excitement and the hair on the back of my nape rose slightly, but I saw nothing new. The road was divided by magic white lines - I told Edwin - which kept our car safely out of the way of advancing cars as we drove through a town.

'Magic white lines?' cried Edwin. 'There's no magic attached to them. Grandma never overtakes that's all, not even a milk float. You know, where they deliver pints of milk in bottles. Or they buy it in the supermarket.'

When I wondered whatever happened to cows Edwin's grandmother told us to keep quiet, we were coming to the clock tower.

'This is an awful roundabout,' she said, stopping the car, watching helplessly as cars whizzed round and past us from all directions.

'The best thing is,' she said, 'to shut your eyes and aim.'

'Only kidding,' she added when Edwin groaned.

'You would have known all this if you hadn't disappeared into yourself when we drove through on our way to Cambridge.'

Cambridge?

'Is it a river with a bridge?' I asked.

It was a town with many bridges, apparently, as well as many colleges.

'Colleges are schools for clever people who like studying,' said Edwin. 'Do you think it could be where Merlin's new magicians are?'

It could be, I said, except Edwin's grandmother said Cambridge wasn't a little fishing village, it was a city because of the colleges even if it not have a cathedral.

'But even cities had to start somewhere,' said Edwin. When his grandmother said he was right, he nearly fell of his seat with excitement; it was the first time his grandmother had said that..

'I do believe my heart is singing,' he said.

So I had to look out for feeling excitement., I thought as we finally managed to cross the road and we left the town. I now saw vast greens on which nervous long-legged and most magnificent horses were exercised by grooms. Then we stopped to let some riders cross the road.

More marvellous horses ridden by grooms.

And very small some of them were.

'Jockeys,' said Edwin's grandmother, opening the car window, 'they race the horses - thoroughbreds all bred from one Arab stallion - according to weight.'

I heard her as through a dense fog.

'Why is this place so good for horses?' I asked faintly.

'It's the position, you see,' she said. 'There are hundreds of acres of good grassland here. It's flat, of course, and these horses we stopped for are off to gallop on the Gallops.'

'Could this be called Suffolk's flatland, and could this have been Exning in the past?' I asked, but alas, no.

'Exning is a small village not far from here. After it was burned down, I believe, they held a new market here, Newmarket, you see, and Newmarket is in Cambridgeshire,' Edwin's grandmother said, 'some parts of it are, anyway.'

'Come to think of it, it might now be in Suffolk,' she added. Unlike the smith, she wsa very fond of words. 'But you know what the powers-that-be are like. They shift boundaries as if there was no tomorrow.'

'There's something else I want to show you presently,' Edwin's grandmother added, driving along a deserted road bordered with grass and hedges without any houses in the near distance. 'It's a small boy's grave looked after by gypsies, somewhere near Risby.'

'And here it is,' she said, drawing up at the side of the road. 'And if there hadn't been a traffic jam I don't suppose we would have seen it.'

She pointed to a jar filled with oxeye daisies and poppies and Edwin and I tumbled out of the car after her.

**

'And here we stop,' Brother Aloysius said.

'Already? Where are we?'

'Somewhere near Risby,' he said, dismounting. I followed him.

A few flowers were wilting in a jar amongst the deep grass.

'I always say a prayer here,' he said. 'Maybe you can freshen up the flowers. There's a little stream yonder.'

It was not yet the season for summer flowers, but I spotted some bluebells and primroses.

'Whose grave is it?' I asked. 'Was it somebody important?'

'Not in the scheme of things,' he said, 'and yet it is. Passers-by keep the grave fresh.'

It was a child who died there, he said, 'no more than three years old.'

**

'Wasn't there a boy who was locked out because he had a disfiguring disease and drowned?' Edwin cried.

Excitement had coloured his eyes nearly as dark a blue as the cornflowers in the jar.

'I think this is the same grave so you have to pick some daisies and put them with the others,' Edwin said.

The loop!

'The loop! Something from the past had connected me to the present, or the other way round,' I said gathering flowers and putting them into the jar just as I had that first time so long ago. Except this time I had to use my psycho-kinetic power (as Edwin's father had called it) and not my hands.

'Whatever is that smell?' Edwin's grandmother asked when I got back into the car.

'Well, it's not me,' said Edwin.

'I should think not. It smells of fresh air and meadows. Anything to do with you, Matthew?'

'It's Morgan le Fey,' I said. 'It's her scent.'

'If it was me, it wouldn't smell of meadows,' Edwin said, sniggering.

She turned the key which started the car - I had worked this out - and then she switched it off again.

'I think a trip to the library is called for,' she said. 'I might get on the blower to your mother first,

212

Edwin.'

She fumbled in her bag.

'And stop giggling like a girl, Edwin. When I was young a telephone was called a blower.'

When she found the blower - a black thing she didn't blow into - she pressed a few numbers.

'Jennifer,' she said. 'How are things?'

She listened.

'Happy? Together? That's good. I'm glad to hear it,' she said. 'In that case I might get my life back one of these days.'

She listened.

'Now don't be like that. I'm just cruel to be kind. You know you and Earl are made for each other. Anyway, I'm taking the boys to Bury library.'

She listened again.

'I know I haven't got a ticket. I don't want to take a book out, we just want to look a few things up. And as for '*boys*', Edwin still has got his imaginary friend as you call him.'

She listened again.

'I know he's a bit old for an imaginary friend, but I'm a lot older and have no imagination whatsoever, and Matthew's my friend too, so what do you make of that?'

For some reason, Edwin not smelling like a meadow and the talk of blowers seemed funnier by the minute. She left the car with the blower to get away from our laughter and had a few more words with Edwin's mother in private.

'Books,' I said when I had calmed down. They had so many books. I had heard of books, different, proper books, of course. Written and illuminated by monks, they were so rare I didn't think even the Saxmunds possessed one.

Edwin was not surprised.

'Even King John, who signed the Magna Carta, was illiterate.'

A new illness, I thought. I hoped it wasn't catching and that he had recovered, but I didn't mention it.

'Yes, books,' said Edwin. 'We'll look in the local history section. The history of Newmarket/Exning is bound to be in there.'

Edwin's grandmother came back into the car

'Onward and upward!' she cried.

Then she drove into town and parked the car.

The library - an imposing red brick building - was a few hundred yards from the car park. Just what would we find out about Exning? I was eager to go and *give it some* as Edwin called it.

Chapter 32

Edwin and I followed his grandmother who strode into the library full of purpose. She looked about her, her head swivelling like an owl looking for prey.

'Now then, Edwin, look sharp. We want the history section.'

He glanced into a large room which was indeed full of books on shelves. He pulled one out and showed it to me. It had no illuminations whatsoever. It was deeply disappointing.

'But they have a computer here,' Edwin announced after a while. 'We might look up Newmarket on a website.'

His grandmother said she didn't believe in computers let alone websites. 'History!' she said, pointing to a sign overhead.

'Aha. Local history.' She removed a book. 'And here it is. Newmarket,' she said, and started to read silently, without moving her lips.

'Listen! Exning,' she read aloud, 'experienced severe floods in thirteen-ninety-three. Blaa-blaah blaah. AHA! Exning suffered extensive fires in the seventeenth century, that must be when the new market came about..'

She turned a few pages.

'Nothing about the Saxmunds in here, I'm afraid,' she said waving the book in the air.

'You read this, Edwin.'

Edwin started to read it.

'*On the road from Bury to Newmarket is Risby which recently commemorated its 1000th anniversary. Eight miles further on the right on the crossroads is an unprotected but always bedecked grave. Here was buried a shepherd*

215

*lad who, accused of stealing a sheep in the
cruel days when such a crime carried the death
penalty, hanged himself.'*

A child of about seven or eight, a curly-headed
blonde girl clutching her mother's hand, looked up at
him.

'Really,' the woman tut-tutted. 'This is most
unsuitable for a child's ears.'

'It is rather shocking,' Edwin's grandmother
said, 'but then so were the times. I don't think it does
any harm to remind a child of how good the times are
now. Carry on Edwin.'

Edwin waited until the girl had been dragged
away by her mother.

*'Ever since, his resting place has been looked
after, it is thought, by gypsies working at night, for
morning reveals a newly tended grave.'*

'Who are these gypsies and why are they called
gypsies?' I asked.

'They are wandering folk, and in the olden days
they were thought to be Egyptians,' said his
grandmother.

Edwin closed the book, an inpatient look on his
face and his grandmother put it back on the shelf.

'It's gypsies now,' he said, 'but it was the grave
Brother Aloysius and Matthew stopped at before that.
That is the loop, I am certain.'

So we had a loop! I was in the mood for more!
But where exactly were they?

'We'll look at the Abbey and then head for Clare
to find more connections,' his grandmother said,
leading the way into town, although I tried to tell her I
had never been to Bury St. Edmunds before. We passed
a most magnificent church which wasn't an Abbey, she
said. 'We'll have to ask somebody,' she said, 'somebody

who looks as if they might know.'

Elderly people, children and their mothers, babies being pushed in small carts were on the pavement.

And then I saw it, a brown habit.

I used my powers to make him stop striding along and tugged fiercely at his habit.

He had brown eyes and a sharp face, rather like Brother Anselm's. Believe it or not, and I could not believe it, I absolutely longed to see that bad-tempered old brother again moaning about his bones.

'Did you do this?' the monk barked at Edwin.

'Do what?' Edwin said.

'Don't play the innocent with me,' he said in a deep voice.

Edwin's grandmother clutched her handbag to her chest.

'Perhaps you have not heard that the meek will inherit the earth,' she said, 'although I'm surprised that you haven't in the trade you are in.'

'I have heard of it,' he said, 'but I don't think *you* will *be* one of the qualifiers, madam.'

She laughed. 'A kindred spirit. Could you kindly inform us where the Abbey is situated?'

He apologised and said yesterday a blond boy with glasses - just like Edwin - had jumped on his toe and he suffered dreadfully with gout.

Like Brother Anselm!

'This is the Frontispiece leading to the Abbey gardens which contains some remains of the lay-out of the Abbey,' he added. 'The Abbey fell into ruins after the dissolution of the monasteries. The Abbey was sold off, and the new owner sold the stones.'

'Blame Henry the Eighth,' he said, and made off.

We wandered round the gardens. Flowers were

tightly massed and glowed jewel-bright in the emerging sun. Oh, it was a clever age! They could foretell the weather and mass flowers as bright as rainbows and command the green grass to stop growing, but I cannot say how fiercely I longed for a fragrant meadow.

Maybe it was the faint scent Morgan le Fey had brought with her that had brought it into my mind.

Whatever it was, I felt more than ever I was neither here nor there as we made our way back to the car.

'It's no good going to Clare if this king, this Henry, closed down the monasteries. I expect the Austin Friary will be in ruins as well. But why would Henry want to close them?' I ' asked.

'He wanted to be King and Pope rolled into one,' Edwin's grandmother said. 'For the power as I understand it.'

'And is he all-powerful?'

'He's dead,' Edwin said. 'It was a long time ago. He had gout as well. He was always shouting "*Mind my leg*", well he did in the film, and he had six wives.'

'Not at the same time, Edwin,' his grandmother said. 'He wanted a male heir, you see, Matthew, to carry on the new Tudor line.'

Whatever that was, and it hadn't done him much good.

As we drove along, I said that the past was all on the library shelves in the history section.

'That's why it's called the past,' Edwin said. 'But only the interesting bits and people make it onto the history shelves.'

'That's right,' his grandmother said. 'History is written by winners.'

I wasn't after a winner, and then I recalled Edwin urging me to look on the world as a giant spider's web when the centre was disturbed. I felt slight vibrations now, as if we were nearing the centre of the disturbance which would fling me back from where I had come from.

A different dimension, Edwin called it.

Merlin had called it the life force.

Now I felt I was getting ever nearer through the vibrations, like a distant joy. Was I mad, or was I foretelling the future?

Chapter 33

'Your mother and father are out,' Edwin's grandmother said to him when we drove up to the house in Whepstead.

Now I had seen so many houses I could spot a difference in Edwin's house, it was surrounded by a lot of land.

'About two acres, and the house is half-timbered. It's Grade II listed,' he said when we got out of the car. 'It's Tudor,' he added.

'From the time of the king who shouted, "Mind my leg"?'

'From the time of is daughter, Elizabeth,' Edwin said. 'The house is dated by the smoke hole. It was before houses had chimneys, you see, and the smoke went out through a hole in the roof.'

I begged him to please, please tell me about it, and we started to giggle.

'The key is left under the doormat, very handy for burglars,' Edwin's grandmother added, tut-tutting as we entered the house. 'Burglars are people who break into your house and steal your belongings. At least you didn't have those in your day.'

How about Eli? Didn't he steal the priests bread and cheese when food had to be worked for so hard? And wasn't one of the Commandments, "*Thou shalt not steal?*"' I said.

'I get your point,' she said. 'Wasn't there one about not coveting your neighbour's oxen?'

'I never did,' said Edwin.

'Nor did I.'

We started to laugh.

'I smell polish,' Edwin said. 'I think dad mentioned they were getting somebody in to help in the house so they had a good clean up before she came.

Mum is a translator and she is starting to work shortly.'

'And not before time,' his grandmother said. 'Her mind is crumbling before my very eyes.'

The longer I knew her, the more she reminded me of Biddy I said to Edwin, who was having a drink sitting by the table on a paved area outside the long open windows of the dining room.

'Oh yes, grandma always has the last word. In fact, she's famous for it,' he said. 'I wasn't very keen at first when she muscled in on our friendship. But have you ever thought what would have happened if we *hadn't gone* to Cambridge with grandma?'

He was right.

She had driven us back through Newmarket where we had found the little lad's grave.

'I might be neither here or there for ever,' I said. 'And then I might not be able to waken the spirit of the knight before his grave was disturbed and his bones exposed for all the world to see.'

Edwin, his grandmother and I were sitting on the chairs outside when his parents came out. His mother was about to sit on my lap when Edwin said Matthew was sitting there, or he had been. 'He's got up now,' he added.

His mother steadied himself on his father.

'Calm yourself, Jennifer,' Edwin's father said.

Then he lit one of his white sticks.

'Calm myself, Earl?'

'Earl? Who is this Earl? I have heard talk about him before. Is that your father's title?'

'His name. You can call anybody anything and they do, especially in America! Duke or Earl or Prince or even King,' Edwin said

Then he shouted, 'WADDAYOUKNOW! EARL! THE NOBLEMAN WHO IS NOT A NOBLEMAN IS MY FATHER!'

His parents sat slumped on the table, watching Edwin running up and down the garden hollering and throwing his arms up into the air, while I was stunned. I had heard Edwin's mother call out Earl, but I was so concerned with Edwin's father's safety that I had failed to make the connection.

'We have found two loops. So we are nearly there,' Edwin's grandmother said..

'Nearly where?' Edwin's mother asked faintly. She was called into the house by their new servant, a sharp-faced, brown-haired woman wearing a colourful apron over a blue dress.

'Is it that Muriel Brownlow?' Edwin's grandmother asked. 'Beware. She suffers from a nasty disease. She can't mind her own business.'

'Now then, Edwin,' his father said in his mellow voice. 'About Matthew. And I'm not saying he is necessarily a bad thing. You have become quite bright and cheerful, well, what I have seen of you.'

'Matthew can do something to convince you he is here, or *neither here or there*, as he calls it,' Edwin said.

'I think not. Don't belittle him by making him do tricks like a performing monkey. He did save me from falling off the ladder,' said his father when Edwin's mother returned.

'I remember that. How long are we going to have the pleasure of this spook?' Edwin's mother asked with a shudder.

I wasn't a spook, Edwin said. 'He is an imprint of his personality, of his former self. And he does not walk around the house quite freely.'

Edwin's grandmother came and said that she had to go home at once. Apparently Edwin's grandfather had a nasty fall when he came out of his workshop. He was carrying a few empty mugs and fell over a flower pot and broke his tibia or his fibia. She never knew the difference, she said, except that they were bones in a leg..

'I shall have to leave at once,' she added.

'Poor granddad,' Edwin said as his grandmother was helped into the car by her daughter. 'Why don't you buy a television and a video recorder so he has something to look at?'

She thought it was a good idea, then she looked at me, and I wondered if I would ever see her again.

'Maybe at Halloween. That is when the last of your riddles will be solved.'

'Thank you for your help,' I said through the open car window. 'I'll talk to you on the blower when I have to say goodbye.'

She promised to write to me.

'I'll send you a letter,' she said.

I wondered why she would do that.

'What letter will that be? An *A?* You could tell me now and save yourself the trouble.'

'I'll send you a note,' she said. 'No, not the sort you sing.'

She laughed and said she would miss me. I would miss her too, I thought, for I felt confident my time here was but short. I thought I had detected a pattern in the riddle, I said.

'What is this pattern?' Edwin asked when we returned to the house and went into the kitchen.

The servant – Muriel - stopped chopping vegetables.

'It's not a pattern, wass-a-matter-wiss-you,' she said looking down her nose. 'I'm not making patterns. I'm making a salad.'

Edwin waved me on silently into the hall.

'The pattern is that you have to be alert. You can't find the answers if you chase them because they have to come to you. You have to recognise them.'

'Which is the same thing, or very nearly,' Edwin said, deeply disappointed.

Edwin's mother had also gone to spend time with his grandfather, she didn't like having me about, and we would watch some television in the sitting room, Edwin said. 'Plenty of time to Halloween.'

The television was a gibberish, garish thing in the corner of the room. Young people with too many gleaming teeth and shining hair rushed about, talked to each other, rushed about again, laughed and rushed about again.

I watched in astonishment while Edwin made some random comments. He was obviously familiar with these giddy creatures

'Do you know these people?'

'No. They're actors. They pretend to be somebody else. They're not real.'

'Hallucinations,' I cried, 'but whose hallucinations are they?'

'It's "*Neighbours*".'

'How do your neighbours' hallucinations get there?'

'From Australia. From down under. No, not under the carpet. Follow me,' he said. 'Let's look at my father's globe in the study.'

He opened the door to the study, where his father was sitting in front of yet another grey box, flashing with an eerie green light this time.

He pointed to a round object with lots of blue colour.

'The blue is the sea, there's more water than sea on Planet Earth.'

He paused.

'The Earth is what is called a Planet, a burnt-out star. This is England,' he said, pointing to an elongated shape,' and, swirling the object around, 'this is Australia. It's because the world is round and travels around the sun. You must be amazed that the earth is round and not flat,' he said, but I wasn't.

'I have never given it a thought,' I said. To be honest, what shape the world was had never been my concern, except when I had to walk uphill.

'When we are near the sun it's day time, when we are away from the sun it's night time and the sun shines somewhere else. And it takes a year for the world to travel around the sun,' he said.

I thought about it deeply.

'So why doesn't a day last for the whole year?'

'It has a daily motion, and a yearly one,' said Edwin, 'but let's forget it.'

'How's your thesis coming along, dad?' he asked.

When his father replied he had a lot more thinking to do, I ventured that nothing could come from nothing.

'Matthew says nothing can come from nothing.'

'Is Matthew an early Greek?'

Edwin shook his head.

'Ask your friend what he means by that.'

'It's God who starts it all. The order of things. Everything has to have a beginning. Like oak trees growing out of acorns.'

Edwin repeated what I said.

'I know where your friend comes from. He comes from the Middle Ages.'

When Edwin said he had thought it was called medieval, his father said it might also be called medieval.

'Matthew is a plague victim on a quest. He crossed over into Camelot and was given tasks and a riddle to solve. Merlin took him and his friends to the place where the ley-lines of Antiquity cross which is over there.'

He pointed to the old yew visible through the study window.

'It's certainly old, it's under a Protection Order, but I thought it was listed as Tudor, like the house. I don't suppose eh...Matthew was told why the Druids built henges, like Stonehenge?'

I knew some of it but far from all, I said.

'Henges were built in Antiquity. I don't believe it was the Druids, but they too believed that an unbroken line, a ring with no ending or beginning, represented nature renewing itself. They made sacrifices but Merlin didn't go into that.'

'How did they move the great stones and erected them into place?'

'Probably with teams of twelve oxen,' I said.

'Of course. It's all very strange, Edwin, you having a ghost friend, but you know what the bard said. *There are more things in heaven and earth, Horatio, than are dreamed of in our philosophy.*'

Edwin put his bad-tempered face on, muttering he hoped *his father wouldn't muscle in on us like grandma had,* as we left him.

'That philosophy thing was Shakespeare,' Edwin said when we reached the kitchen.

'Shakespeare?' cried Muriel, who was busy going through Edwin's mother's handbag, spilling the contents when we startled her.

'I've heard of him. And Shakespeare wasn't any good until that apple fell on his head.'

She tried to push everything back into the bag.

'You don't look a happy bunny to me, Edwin,' she said to distract him.

'I'm not,' he said. 'And why are you going

226

through my mother's handbag?'

'She left it behind when she rushed off after your grandmother. And I just thought I check in case she needed anything,' Muriel said lamely. 'But I didn't know she took pills for depression,' she added, shaking a small box. 'It just goes to show. Living in this lovely place. Money to burn, a considerate husband, and she's taking pills for depression.'

'She's better now,' Edwin said, taking the pills. 'St John's Wort,' he read slowly.

'It's an anti-depressant,' Muriel said.

St John's Wort. Green leaves, dotted with tiny translucent spots, carrying their yellow flower heads like crowns. Biddy had used it to calm me down, and Edwin's mother used it for depression.

'ST JOHN'S WORT FOR DEPRESSION!' Edwin screamed, jumping up and down, 'ST JOHN'S WORT FOR DEPRESSION!'

'On second thoughts I'm not surprised your mother takes them. It can't be nice having a son who is not all there,' Muriel said.

Depression was a low spirit, Edwin said, a low spirit like the Lady Isabel had suffered from, I said after we left the kitchen, overjoyed at finding the second loop -St. John's Wort- connecting the present to the past.

I just had to get on the blower to Edwin's grandmother and tell her.

Edwin went into the hall. He pressed some numbers and handed me the blower which I put to my ear. When I asked what I had to say, he said to tell his grandmother who I was first.

'Yes?' a voice said when the bells stopped.

'Who is it?'

'I am Matthew, the cooper's son. Can you tell Edwin's grandmother we have discovered another connection?'

Edwin took the thing away from me and I went into the garden. It was very difficult talking to somebody who you couldn't see, and for the very first time I understood just how hard it was for Edwin's parents, *who could neither see me or hear me*.

I wasn't there as far as they were concerned, and yet I was for Edwin.

If I missed my cut-off date I would be duty-bound to leave this family to live their own lives. What would I do then?

I sat under the apple tree that had been full of white blossoms when I first saw Edwin. It was now full of yellow apples turning rosy where the sun caught them.

I was not a happy bunny, as Muriel would say.

Edwin joined me as darkness fell. He was not a happy bunny either.

'Parents,' he said. 'Who would have them.'

Chapter 34

'Parents,' Edwin repeated. 'You couldn't guess what they have cooked up for me now.'

He held up his hands.

'I mean what they are planning to do in the autumn. Fall, dad calls it. He's just told me. First we're having a Halloween party, a fancy-dress party, I knew that, but after that we are going to *America* until next June.'

He paused.

'I don't mind going for a holiday,' he said.

Holidays -not Holy Days- were a mystery to me after Edwin's explanation. People left their homes, for no good reason, one or two or three times a year. They inhabited another house and then they returned. However many houses did they want?

'Mum and dad can work from there,' said Edwin, 'and I will have to go to school with my cousin Ethan in Sugarland, in Texas. They're scientists and work for an oil company. That's where my other grandparents and my aunt and uncle and the cousins live.'

'Don't you like your other grandparents and your cousins? And don't you want a party?'

He said he wanted a party but he wasn't sure about America.

'My grandparents are sort of weird. My grandfather is very stern and just wants everybody to have straight 'A' grades.'

'Doesn't everybody,' I cried.

Edwin laughed.

'My grandmother doesn't like to be alone and has masses of people to dinner. Mum says she grabs passing strangers. And my cousin Ethan is just like my father, impossibly clever. My father majored in History when he was twenty-one,' he said.

'Is this where he learned to ride the clouds?'

'He went to a military academy after that and then into the air force.'

He put his discontented face on, the one with the frowning forehead.

'But mum and dad never ask me *what I want to do,*' he added, 'they just tell me.'

It might be because he was still a child and not out and about in the world, I said.

'Maybe, and that awful Muriel person is looking after our house until we get back.'

Muriel was certainly dumb. She had talked about '*money to burn*'. I recalled the Florin Alec gave me. Try burning that!

I knew it couldn't be done, no good asking about it, so I asked him what a fancy-dress party was.

Edwin laughed.

'I'm so relieved! For a moment I thought I would have to explain America to you. You see, it was discovered a hundred years later.'

Later than what? I wondered, but I didn't ask him, I didn't have time for lengthy explanations, I now had to endure a fancy-dress party; at a fancy-dress party people pretended to be somebody else.

'Like the hallucinations on the gibberish box?'

He shook his head.

'We are the same but we wear different clothes. On Halloween it's mostly skeletons and spooks, remember MERLIN'S FLYING SPOOKS?'

'Spooks are scary, but you are my friend,' I told him.

He paused.

'We are more than friends, we are brothers, and I would make a sacrifice for you.'

Edwin? Making a sacrifice for me?

'Promise?'

He promised.

.   'This party. I'm going as...you guess.'

'This King Henry the Tudor with the bad leg?'

He shook his head.

'Sir William of Saxmund?'

'An Austin friar.'

'Brother Aloysius?'

'No, Brother Anselm,' he said. 'Then I can be as rude to everybody as I want.'

With this happy thought he went to bed.

I stayed in the garden. Edwin seemed to think I would be released on Halloween. but I wasn't too sure.

Halloween was still some weeks ahead, but I felt a slight pull as I looked at a pale moon and inhaled the scent of meadows.

I called out to Morgan le Fey and I asked her for a favour once I was gone.

She didn't answer me but I knew she was about

'I want feathery grasses and daisies and clover and poppies and cornflowers for Edwin to see what a meadow is,' I called out. 'And purple loosestrife,' I added more softly in case she asked me what they were like. I liked the name but I had no idea what sort of flowers they were.

Saturday was uneventful. Edwin slept late. His father was in the study. I would have liked to watch the hallucinations after he went to bed and in the morning, but I had promised to wait for Edwin to switch them on for me.

'Your energy could be too strong for the set,' he said. 'And some of the things shown after the watershed -no, it doesn't have water or a shed- would be too much for you.'

We slunk about the house and looked for connections through listening to Muriel and Edwin's dad's conversations. They were mostly about Edwin's granddad's broken leg which had been set and was on the mend, and then his mother came back.

'We won't find the last answer to the riddle until Halloween, - All Souls' Day - because it's your birthday,' Edwin said confidently. 'I might make a start and write down your life story. 'Or perhaps not,' he added, so we watched the hallucinations. Television, I should say.

It was amusing, especially when I got the story. I didn't understand the ones which involved a ball being hit, kicked or bashed, but I liked the crowds of people being so very happy about it. Their hearts were probably singing. I loved something new, and in my day it had mostly been the changing seasons.

I couldn't get enough of it, but that Sunday morning - the thirtieth of August as it said on the screen - it was sad.

It was about a princess.

I could tell she was a princess. She wore a small crown on her golden hair. She was beautiful and had wondrous blue eyes.

Everybody stared at her, amazed at her beauty.

There were lots of other pictures of her without crowns.

I liked the one where she ran with open arms towards her two boys.

I understood the story which made out this beautiful princess had died.

'This story is a bit sad,' I said to Edwin, who sat there open-mouthed.

'I wonder what the ending will be,' I said.

He got up.

'DAD!' he screamed. 'Here, DAD!'

His father came running out of his study.

'Princess Diana has died in a car accident,'

Edwin said.

'I don't believe it,' his father said. He sat down and watched as more sad and probably important people talked about the princess.

'I shall have to tell Muriel, and I must telephone your grandmother, Edwin,' he said. 'She will be upset.'

Muriel was in the kitchen. She was crying and sniffling into a tea towel.

'Is this real?' I asked Edwin.

He nodded.

'Princess Diana is not a story,' he said.

'I should think not,' Muriel said. 'Princess Diana is not a story indeed. I think you're the most stupid boy I ever came across.'

It was a real princess who had been married to a real prince who was the son of a real queen. Princess Diana had two boys. One was blond and handsome. The other boy was red-haired. He had a determined air of charm which reminded me of Jacob.

The princess had lived alone in a palace called Kensington.

All week people placed flowers at the palace gates, so many flowers, great mounds of flowers, all the flowers of the land, with notes attached to each bunch, and at night they lit candles and wandered about outside the palace, lost and weeping.

I didn't understand much about the princess's life except that many, many people had loved her.

'Almost everybody,' Edwin said. 'My mum did because she was Princess Diana, I suppose. She showed them and knocked them for six with her glamour. Like in cricket. A stroke to the boundary is worth six runs. Never mind that. My dad liked her because...I'll ask him. DAD! CAN YOU COME HERE FOR A MINUTE?'

Edwin's father came in quietly. Edwin asked

him why he liked her and he said Princess Diana had a great humanity.

'Ask him to name it,' I said.

Edwin's father thought about it.

'She showed great compassion to the children and the sick,' he finally said, 'so you could say she had a sweet benevolence.'

A sweet benevolence. By naming it, it became recognisable.

The funeral.

It was held on the hallucinations so all the country could see it.

At the start, the important ladies dressed in black stood in a huddle. They were not allowed to walk behind the horse-drawn coffin which was draped by a flag.

It must have been hard for the boys walking behind it with the other important men of the family but they were very brave about being stared at by the multitude.

A multitude had been mentioned once by Brother Aloysius, but that was the first time I had seen one. I had imagined it to be noisy but it was a silent and sad multitude.

We watched the funeral all day, Edwin and I, his father, his mother, and Muriel. As I understood it they didn't know Princess Diana personally, but they acted as if they shared the sorrow falling onto the land.

It was during the speeches made in the great Abbey that I became upset for Edwin and his parents.

It was clear to me they would have to take sides as the two noble houses of Windsor and Spencer were two warring families.

I had to warn Edwin about the dangers, so I

beckoned him to follow me into the garden, but he told me not to get agitated. There wouldn't be a civil war.

'Isn't the king the nation now?'

'We have a queen. She's important but she's mostly only a figurehead,' he said.

It was probably a good thing if it stopped civil war breaking out, I decided following Edwin back into the house.

I meant to go into the living room with him but instead I was compelled to linger in the hall.

I could not leave it.

Edwin had said the world was like a giant spider's web, I would be flung into a different dimension, and now the spider's threads wound themselves round my legs and held me there with silken threads.

I wished to bid Edwin farewell with all my heart, but I could not move.

Nothing happened for a while.

Then Edwin's grandmother rang and Edwin's mother came into the hall and I heard her discuss the funeral with Edwin's grandmother.

'Apparently Diana will not be interred in the Spencer family crypt. She'll be buried on an island in the lake,' Edwin's mother said. 'It strikes me be as quiet odd. I mean she'll be another *Lady in the Lake*.'

I wanted to call out to Edwin, but I couldn't find my voice.

Edwin's mother stopped talking and she listened.

'You're absolutely right, mother,' she said. 'All those wonderful flowers to remember her by. I've never seen so many in my life. You could truly say she made THE LAND BLOOM.'

THE NEW LADY IN THE LAKE WHO MADE THE LAND BLOOM! The new legend.

235

'Just so,' said a whispering voice. 'There can be no beginnings without endings.'

'What is the ring,' I asked Morgan le Fey.

'It is the ring of history. There has to be an end, and then a beginning, the start of a new legend joins the old legend closes the ring. You have carried out your tasks and solved the riddles.'

'Summon Edwin,' I said. 'I have to say farewell.'

'I will try, but my time is done. By making a meadow for you I have nearly used up what little strength I had left.'

The voice was now a sigh in the wind.

'But tell the boy Edwin, who has called you his brother, it is only through letting you go that the ring will be closed and that he will find you again,' Morgan le Fey said, and then she was gone.

BOOK 2:

THE WARRIOR'S SON

Chapter 35

An intense light and heat followed a loud explosion.

The television screen went blank, and Edwin's father rushed to the window and looked at the garden.

'Good Lord,' he said. 'Look at that. The yew tree has been struck by lightning. It's completely demolished.'

'Lightning doesn't strike out of a clear blue sky,' Edwin cried. 'And it's not just outside. There's a strange light in here as well.'

'Stay indoors, Edwin, it might be dangerous,' his mother cried, but he ignored her.

He followed the bright light which was moving slowly from the house into the garden, all the while looking up at it.

'Don't leave me yet, Matthew,' he cried. 'Please don't. It's too soon. I'm not ready for it! I'll let you go when the time comes! I swear I will! There's still three weeks to All Souls Day! Merlin can't have got it wrong!'

But there was only a deep silence. Edwin had heard that silence before.

He had heard it when his parents had separated, and then again at Princess Diana's funeral.

The absence of sound was the silence of loss.

Edwin rushed outside; the yew tree had gone. It was as if Matthew hadn't come from it to find him crying.

Matthew was suspended over this emptiness in a faint bubble.

Edwin could still see him clearly, his dark hair and eyes, his breeches and white shirt and waistcoat, the blue ribbon of time holding his ponytail.

'Don't be sad, Edwin,' he whispered, 'let me go. 'You have to make the sacrifice you promised. My time has come.'

'Not yet it hasn't,' cried Edwin.

'My time has come sooner than we thought, but we were more than friends, we were brothers. You said so yourself,' Matthew whispered. 'Say the words and set me free. If you let me go you will find me again.'

'Rubbish! Once you're gone you're gone! And I might have said we were brothers, but you can't go yet. It's TOO SOON.'

'Now is the time to say the words.'

'Why don't you listen? It's TOO SOON. It's not Halloween yet. Nobody ever tells me anything. Just do it, they say. You're just like everybody else.'

He paused.

'I don't know what words to say. I suppose I could find out if I wanted to from my notes, but I don't want to.'

'It won't be too much for you.'

Edwin looked at him.

'Please yourself,' he said. 'You're just another disappointment.'

Then he turned his back and walked to the house, tears streaming down his face.

The power was back on inside. The television was blaring from the sitting room and the 'phone was ringing.

It was his grandmother.

'What happened?' she asked.

'I don't want to talk about it,' he said and put the 'phone down. 'I want to be alone.'

If there was such a place.

Dad wanted to talk to him about Matthew, Muriel wanted to talk about the explosion, and his mother wanted to talk - of all things - about meadows.

He curled his lip and went up to his bedroom where he was drawn to the window.

Matthew was still there, floating in his bubble.

'Serves you right!'

He threw himself onto his bed when his hands curled around the pillow and he felt something and heard a faint crackling.

His notes!

He sat up and put his glasses on and started to read.

FIND THE HEART OF THE SPIDER'S NET.

1) Your mother gave up her warm cottage and had this cough.
2) The Blessed Abbot renounced his wealth.
3) Mary under the cross gave up her son.
4) Remember what made the wasteland bloom.
5) Sir Galahad fell down dead.
6) Your father left the village to find the lost boy.
7) You had to go to the blacksmith.

There was no getting away from it. The important word was staring him in the face but he ignored it and concentrated on Matthew instead. Matthew had answered the final question of the riddle, but what was it?

He had disappeared *without telling him*. He crept into his parents' bedroom and rang his grandmother.

'I suppose Matthew's gone sooner than we thought, that was what the commotion was all about,' she said. 'We are sad but we should be happy.'

'You sound like the Queen.'

'Some chance,' she said, and he always had his memories to cheer him up.

'But I want new memories,' he said. 'What exactly did mum say to you?'

'She said Princess Diana would be another

Lady in the Lake. And she talked about the flowers, how the land bloomed.'

'The land blooming, that was the last connecting loop!' Edwin cried, putting the 'phone down.

Matthew's task on earth was completed. Now he had to carry out the task in *Neitherland* and wake up the knight's spirit so that he, Mattie and Frog and the children could reach the *Hereafter*.

If I will let Matthew go he will have his friends Mattie and Frog and I will be alone, but I just might do it, Edwin thought. Immediately a nagging worry wriggled in his brain like a worm. What if he couldn't find the right words to say?

The words in the list were easy. SACRIFICE.

It wasn't a word Edwin was used to but Matthew had sacrificed himself so he could wake up the knight. So he ought to do the same and say the words and let him go, but then sacrifice was probably easier for Matthew. He was more used to it coming from medieval times, or was it perhaps a more grown-up thing to do?

He could easily be grown-up if he wanted to be, Edwin thought, very easily, except sacrifice wasn't just a word, it was something you did.

He felt an overwhelming urge to grab at something, to anchor himself, for somebody to help him, when he recalled the closing words of the riddle: OVERCOME SADNESS AND CLOSE THE RING.

These words, Morgan Le Fey's words, were directed at him, at Edwin, the warrior's son.. He had better behave like it.

The Ring wasn't closed until he let Matthew go. He let himself silently out of the house and ran down the garden towards the place where the yew tree used to be.

He looked up at Matthew, suspended in his bubble.

He wanted to say the words to let Matthew go, but what were they?

He raised his arms, and when he did he knew the answer.

'The Brotherhood.
In Life.
In Death.'

Matthew smiled and opened his mouth as if he wanted to say something, but before he could he melted into the air.

It was a weird evening.

The atmosphere of the funeral, the shock of the explosion and the close proximity of the supernatural coloured everybody's mood, although Edwin merely missed Matthew, it was as simple as that.

Making sacrifices and being grown-up wasn't all it was cracked up to be. On top of his pain his parents treated him like a baby.

They asked him in soft voices w

hat he wanted for dinner, should they take out a video, would he like a game of football in the garden, should Jonathan come over.

Edwin - newly grown up - warded off all suggestions with a polite 'No thank you, it's very kind of you,' although he wanted to shout, 'why can't you leave me alone?'

His mother told Muriel to make Edwin a chocolate fudge cake.

'Not today I won't,' Muriel said. 'I'm not touching anything electrical.'

She shivered.

'Chocolate cake indeed. You don't know you're born,' she said to Edwin.

She took her apron off, put on her coat and went to get her bicycle.

The days had shortened. It was already dark outside but Muriel shook her head when Edwin's father's offered to run her home.

'I've got my trusty steed,' she said.

Edwin found the bicycle he hadn't used in a while and cycled with her through the dark village lanes to the next village where she lived.

He rode in front to shield her from the sudden glare of the odd oncoming car's blinding headlights.

A bright moon cast dark shadows from the trees onto the road.

'We'll be like ET and ride over the treetops across the moon,' he shouted back at her.

'Who?'

'The Extra-Terrestrial.'

She hoped Edwin wasn't going silly again, she said, then she turned right and stopped in front of a pretty cottage.

Edwin waited until she had let herself into the house before he cycled home, putting his bike into the shed rather than leaving it in a heap on the gravel path.

He paused and looked into the living room where his mother and father sat on the settee beneath a pool of light cast from a lamp.

They were looking at books.

His mother did technical translations from German into English. Maybe she was stuck, he thought, but she wasn't.

'Your mother has a fancy for a proper meadow,' said his father. 'We're just looking it up.'

'That's right,' she said. 'And the first part is easy. You just let the grass grow long. Then you drill some seeds into the ground.'

'The grass will grow when we're in America I expect,' Edwin said. 'You can do the seed-thing when we come back.'

His mother leaned against her father.

'It's not only the look of a meadow which attracts me. It's gone now, but I have noticed its scent for quite a while now.'

'Well it wasn't me,' Edwin said.

He laughed when he went upstairs, Grandma was right; he did have his memories.

When his father came up and sat on his bed he ruffled his hair as if he was a baby.

'Just imagine yourself returning to earth in six-hundred years' time. It would be a very different, strange, unrecognisable place. Maybe alien or maybe primitive, who knows? Wouldn't you be pleased to find a friend who helped you? You must have been lonely if your only friend was a ghost-boy.'

'But I loved him! I secretly hoped we wouldn't solve the last question of the riddle and we would have been friends forever.'

'You mean friends as equals, I suppose. But the relationship would have changed as you grew older. You would become a man and Matthew would still be a boy.'

His father was right.

It was time to stop living for themselves and get out into the wide world, his father added. Grandpa had a stroke. It was minor, but he wasn't all that well, and Edwin's cousin Ethan was in a lot of trouble.

The perfect Ethan in trouble!

Edwin was delighted, but only for a moment.

'He's been expelled from school,' his father said, for writing rude things about his teacher in a text book..

Now that was not something Ethan would do, but it was awful. Everybody knowing he had misbehaved on top of Grandpa's stroke! And then Edwin's mind turned towards America.

'I don't remember that much about Sugarland. I know everything's big but I didn't think it was that marvellous with it being so hot and being inside all the time.'

His father laughed.

'Neither do I, but it's a start.'

Making a start seemed to be the important thing, Edwin thought.

Probably.

He was awake for a long time but finally drifted off into a dream-filled sleep. He was in a large house with many rooms. Every door he opened revealed a brightly lit furnished room, all bar one which was dark.

I have to make a start and find out what's in there, he thought, desperately trying to part the dark with his hands, and suddenly he was cycling with Matthew the cooper's son to the Friary in Clare through dark country lanes faintly illuminated by the swaying lights of their bicycle lamps.

'This machine is indeed a trusty steed,' Matthew cried pedalling madly, his hair blowing in the wind.

'I wonder what Brother Anselm will have to say when we get to Clare.'

'You're bicycle thieves. I'll have no truck with bicycle thieves,' Matthew cried, fading into the light.

Edwin woke with a start, then he closed his eyes again. It felt so good cycling with Matthew that he wanted it to go on forever, but instead he fell into a dreamless sleep.

When he woke up, his grandmother was sitting on his bed.

'Grandma! Have you materialised?'

'Chance would be a fine thing with your grandfather thinking only men can drive a car. I'm here because I've got some news for you,' she said. 'As the day will start whether you get up or not, you might as well get up and hear it.'

'What's your news?' Edwin asked jumping out of bed.

'It's about the bones they have unearthed on the air bas in Lakenheath.'.

'The one under the baseball pitch? Whose grave is it?'

His grandmother held her hands up.

'I don't know. But archaeologists are working on it. It might well be be on the East Anglian News, I expect.'

'I'll be in America when it's broadcast,' Edwin finished for her glumly.

'That's right,' she said. 'But as I said to your grandfather only last night, isn't it a good job you finally got the hang of setting the video machine?'

Was the grave relevant to his dreams, he wondered? but now it was time to live in the real world, as his father had told him.

He wanted to do something to say thank you to his grandmother. He got washed and dressed and went downstairs into the kitchen where grandma was making coffee for everybody.

He was at the sink, filling a bucket with water, when Muriel came in.

'Morning Miss Brownlow. Come on your trusty steed?' he said. 'I won't be long at the sink. I'm just going to wash grandma's car.'

He left the kitchen very carefully so he wouldn't spill any water.

Neither his grandmother or Muriel Brownlow

247

were religious women, but they almost crossed
themselves.

Chapter 36

It was June already.

Time simply flew by, Muriel Brownlow often told herself, and now the Conroys would be back from America within the hour.

She would be glad to see them again, for a little while anyway. They had been good to her, and as for Edwin, now he had turned overnight into a sensible boy. All that craziness had simply vanished.

She was also sorry to see them in a way.

She liked having the house to herself, cycling to her cottage sometimes to keep the home fires burning.

Muriel Brownlow might have liked living by herself and enjoying her own company, but that didn't mean she didn't want to know what was going on. She was still inquisitive. Plain nosey, in fact.

When Edwin's grandmother had come over with a letter and a package for Edwin a fortnight since she hadn't been able to help herself.

'Mrs. Matthews,' she had said, looking at the letter and the package in a larger envelope laying on the dresser. 'Mrs Matthews, I can't help noticing you haven't sealed down the envelopes.'

'So?'

'I once overheard somebody saying I had a nasty disease, I couldn't mind my own business,' Muriel said.

'It can happen to the best of us,' Edwin's grandmother said.

She stuck out her tongue, not at Muriel but to lick the envelope before she stuck them down.

'And another thing,' Muriel Brownlow said. 'I believe I have mentioned to you the grass and weeds before now. I believe they have grown into what you would call a right mess.'

'A meadow,' Edwin's grandmother cried.

She had noticed it when she came in, and wasn't it marvellous? All those feathery grasses and white daisies and pink clovers and blue cornflowers and red poppies swaying in the wind and surrounding the old house.

When she said wouldn't Matthew be pleased, Muriel Brownlow wondered if she meant her husband, except would somebody be called Matthew Matthews?She corrected Mrs. Matthews and said she probably meant Edwin.

'And Edwin, of course,' Edwin's grandmother said going to the window.

'What are those things?' Edwin's grandmother said, pointing to the place where the yew tree used to be, a space now covered in tall flowers glowing like purple candles in the distance.

'Purple loosestrife, I believe,' Muriel said. 'And they are most definitely weeds. They grow on waste-ground, grassland and cleared woodlands, that sort of thing. I hope the family won't mind, nothing was said about me keeping the garden tidy.'

The family didn't mind, in fact they were delighted, especially Edwin and another boy.

Edwin kept jumping up and down, crying, 'Purple Loosestrife,' over and over. So much so that Muriel Brownlow thought his silliness had come back through jet-lag and gave him the envelopes his grandmother had left for him.

'Thanks,' he said with but the faintest of American drawls. 'It's very kind of you. And by the way, this is my cousin Ethan, he is joining us for the summer holidays.'

'Ethan? What a peculiar name. Is that a boy or a

girl?'

'Does he look like a girl?' Edwin cried, and indeed, he didn't. Ethan was tall, and he had a red crew-cut.

'He's a bit older than Edwin,' his mother said coming into the room. 'They're great friends now,' as the boys disappeared.

'I must say you've kept everything beautifully, Miss Brownlow,' she added. 'It's very hot over there, you know. It's wonderful to simply walk around the garden and wallow in all that glorious fresh air.'

Her husband walked in before Muriel had a chance to wallow.

He carried a baby, a girl by the looks of things, Muriel noticed, who was looking around with amazed, blue eyes.

Just as always, thought Muriel, nobody ever told her anything. And just where did they think the baby was going to sleep? when a delivery van drew up.

'Where do you want the cot and the baby bath?' he asked her.

'In the house, where else?' she said.

Cousin Ethan, who had been accused of writing rude things about a teacher in a text book in red ink -except he never used red ink- was back at school. He said he had trouble believing Edwin's story about Matthew, the knight, the tasks and the riddle.

'I'm not disbelieving you, Edwin,' he said running his fingers through his carroty crew-cut. 'It's easier picturing it in your countryside.'

Nobody walked or cycled in Texas. Everything happened inside something; in large air-conditioned houses, in large air-conditioned cars, in large air-conditioned hypermarkets.

He sat down by Edwin's computer.

'Just tell me again how it all started, and I'll type it.'

'If you name something it becomes real. Merlin said that. Or something like it, . Edwin said.

He held up his hand and Ethan listened.

He had the beginning, he said, and Ethan started to type; 'I AM MATTHEW, THE COOPER'S SON.'

'Grandma saw him,' said Edwin.

With that thought, Edwin opened his grandmother's letter.

> *'Dear Edwin,*
>
> *I'll keep this short and won't tell you all about the on-going trauma we had with your grandfather's leg which took rather a long time to heal. I shall tell you all about it when I see you, so you needn't think you have got off lightly.*
>
> *I told your grandfather to make sure to set the machine properly. Your grandfather has `recorded the right programme, it is a news item from About Anglia, it is short because the video wasn't timed right, but it concerns a certain First Knight..'*
>
> > *Love*
> > *Grandma*

Edwin's hand almost shook as he inserted the cassette into the video recorder.

An Anglo-Saxon grave in a US Air Force Base in Suffolk has revealed remains of a warrior in full battle regalia alongside the bodies of his horse and children. The grave was in the manner of a ring, with the knight and horse at its centre. The knight's wooden shield and his sword, the horse's bronze and silver decorated bridle and elongated shield were apparently well preserved.

Archaeologists are currently working on the site…

And here the video stopped.

Edwin stopped breathing for a minute.

'I know I'm right, Ethan. It's the dark room of my dreams made light. Matthew freed the warrior's spirit just before his bones were taken away for all the world to see and lead the children into the *Hereafter.* '

'How about the round burial?'

Edwin could not prove it and never would, but he had no need of it. His knowledge came from the heart; it was in the manner of the Round Table, of the Brotherhood, that the children's small graves surrounded that of the knight.

Edwin thought of the knight, a descendant of the Knight Errants of the Round Table who had roamed the world for adventure, Lancelot's Anglo-Saxon descendant. It had fallen to Matthew, the cooper's son, a descendant -but not the last- of Lancelot, to free his spirit.

Edwin, the boy who had always grumbled that nobody told him anything and everybody muscled in on his territory had grown up since the time he had made a sacrifice and let Matthew go. He had overcome sadness and closed the ring.

But just for a minute he wished he wasn't sitting in his bedroom with the evening sun blazing through his windows but that he was once more crying by the apple tree under a watery blue April sky.

Just for a minute he wished he would set eyes again for the first time on Matthew materialising out of the old yew tree, but first times never repeated themselves.

And then he remembered Matthew saying, 'You will only find me if you let me go.'

Edwin had set him free and now he had the summer to show Ethan where everything had happened. It would be a good project. Maybe that was the way Matthew would return, maybe not.

And there was the purple loosestrife where the yew tree used to be, Mathew's and Mattie's and Frog's burial place. When the flowers faded, he would plant bright flowers on it, Matthew had liked bright colours, especially blue.

It was a beginning. Hadn't Morgan le Fey herself said there could be no beginnings without endings?

Epilogue

Whepstead, Suffolk, 2010

In June, Edwin, an archaeologist engaged to an American girl and on a dig in Turkey, was coming home for an important visit. He and his family - including Grandma - were leaving England for America.

Before the house was put up for sale, Edwin had to oversee an important task; Matthew, Mattie and Frog's remains had to be transferred to a cemetery.

His thirteen-year-old sister, Helena, had picked flowers from the meadow and placed them on the table. His father, a tutor at the University of East Anglia, and his mother, as well as his grandmother, a widow, and Muriel Brownlow, who had made a chocolate fudge cake, were pressing their noses to the window when a taxi stopped at the end of the drive.

A young man got out. Edwin was tall, blond and sunburnt and he carried a bouquet of blue flowers.

'Delphiniums, I believe, Matthew always did like the colour blue, just like Edwin's grandfather, rest his soul,' said Edwin's grandmother.

'Who is Matthew?' asked Muriel Brownlow, but no answer came.

Edwin ran up the drive and placed the flowers amongst a patch of purple loosestrife, glowing in the sunlight. He paused for a moment and then he walked up to the house.

'If it must be done, it will be done by me,' he said. 'I have learnt how to respect ancient burials, I don't want strangers to disturb their grave.'

Their final resting place in the graveyard would be safe. A headstone would say, '*Here rest Mattie, Frog and Matthew, The Cooper's Son.*'